NAME-a-MiTHYaDiSH CONTEST WINNERS!

Hey earthkins!

We ran a contest for naming a N...
(see www.taranauts.com for more...
of names, and they were all winne...
picked as THE one.

THE WINNING NAME FOR THE DISH:

GLO BY CHOCOLATE

AND THE EMPERAZA OF DISH NAMERS:

Nihaal George, 12, Inventure Academy, Bangalore

***

THE WINNERS IN OTHER CATEGORIES!
Most Out-of-the-Box:
The G.P.S. (also known as the Glo-pillo Sandwich)
—Nabeel Tauheed, 13, Loyola School, Jamshedpur

Most Number of Entries:
68! — Abhyuday Atal and Neil Kagalwala, 10, Indus International
School, Hyderabad

Also Scrumpilicious:
From earthkins:
* CHOCSTASY — Nikita George, 8, Inventure Academy, Bangalore
* CHOCKACIOUS MASTASY — Dharitri Chaudhuri, 11, Garden High
School, Kolkata

* **TARAGEMOCO** — D. Vaishnavi, 15, Chennai
* **TARA-FFIC GLO CAKE** — Urvish Paresh Mehta, 15, St.Francis
D'Assisi High School, Mumbai
* **TARACHOCOSCREAM** — Mohit Panjwani, 6, Hiranandani Foundation
School, Thane (W)
* **TARALICIOUS PILLOFUDGE** — Lovely, 14, Patna
* **CHOCOZPONGIE** — Karishma Dhingra, Welham Girls' School,
Dehra Dun
* **DELUMPTIOUS TARADELITE** — V. Annapurani, Chennai
* **MITHARA SNOLUMPIE, MITHAYI** — Neil, Abhyuday, Varun, Anish, 10,
Indus International School, Hyderabad

From older earthkos:
* **PUDGY PILE O' PILLOS** — Shachii Manik, Mumbai
* **MAZEDAARUMTARUM** — Divya Daswani, Chennai

We hope you enjoy making, serving and gobbling up Glo by
Chocolate as much as we do! Oh, and our mastastic fourth
adventure too!

TARANAUTS ZARPA, ZVALA, AND TUFAN

PS: Thank you, Bangalore chefkins Malika Kapadia, 10, Raina
Kapadia, 7, both of Headstart Montessori, Sanjana Rao, 9, TISB,
and Rohan, 8, NPS Indiranagar, for helping us figure out the earth
ingredients for the dish! (Look out for your surprizes!)

* THE EMPERAZA OF DISH NAMERS GETS
BOOKS WORTH RS 1500 + TARANAUTS
SUPERSTUFF FROM HACHETTE INDIA

* ALL WINNERS GET A GIFT HAMPER FROM
HACHETTE INDIA + TARANAUTS POSTER +
MOUSEPAD + BADGES

* ALL PARTICIPANTS GET SURPRIZES!

taranauts

THE RACE FOR THE
gLO
RUBieS

For Leo,
with best wishes,
Roopa Pai

CHASE THE STARS AT
www.taranauts.com

Roopa Pai suspects she has alien blood, for two reasons. One, she loved history in school. And two, although an adult, she mostly reads children's books.

Roopa has won a Children's Book Trust award for science writing. Among her published works are a four-book science series, *Sister Sister* (Pratham Books), and two girl-power books, *Kaliyuga Sita* and *Mechanic Mumtaz* (UNICEF).

When she is not dreaming up plots for her stories, she goes on long solo bicycle rides, and takes children on history and nature walks in Bangalore. You can find her at *www.roopapai.in*.

taranauts
BOOK FOUR

THE RACE FOR THE
GLO
RUBIES

Roopa Pai

Illustrated by Priya Kuriyan

hachette
INDIA

First published in 2011 by Hachette India

www.hachetteindia.com

10 9 8 7 6 5 4 3 2 1

ISBN: 978-93-80143-54-5

Hachette India
612/614 (6th Floor), Time Tower
MG Road, Sector 28, Gurgaon 122001, India

Typset in Perpetua 13.5/16 by
Eleven Arts, New Delhi

Printed and bound in India by
Manipal Press Ltd, Manipal

For Ak Ka and Tam Ma,
You keep me centred.

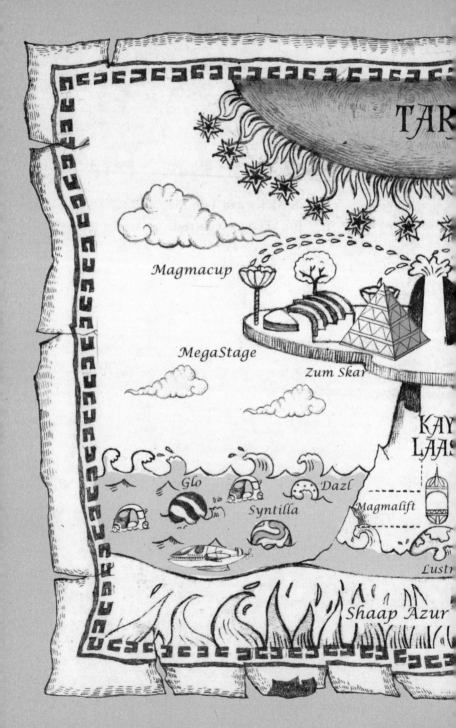

TAR

Magmacup

MegaStage

Zum Skar

KAY
LAAS

Glo

Dazl

Syntilla

Magmalift

Lustr

Shaap Azur

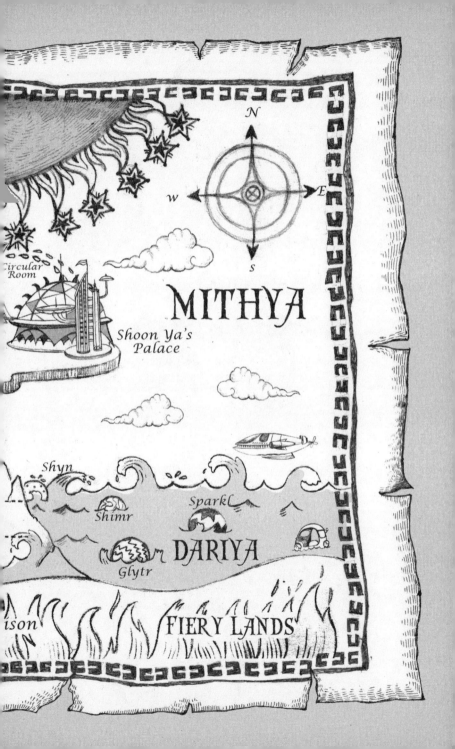

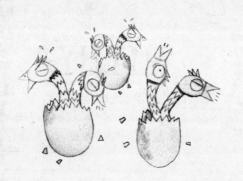

Taranauts
The Trail of the Tale

Eight octons after the wise, brave Shoon Ya became Emperaza of Mithya, Mithya was celebrating with the grandest Octoversary ever. For the first time, the 32 stars of Tara—the supersun with the cool rainbow coloured light—had come down to dance at the celebrations. But their dance was rudely interrupted by Shoon Ya's evil twin, Shaap Azur, who broke out of his prison below the heaving seabed of Dariya and captured all 32 stars in the Silver Spinternet, plunging Mithya into darkness.

The stars could be rescued, but only if the 32 riddles Shaap Azur had hidden on the eight worlds were solved within an octet. Enter sweet-faced Zvala, child of Fire, athletic Zarpa, child of the SuperSerpent Shay Sha, and animal magnet Tufan, child of the Wind—three gifted mithyakins who had been chosen by the Emperaza several octons ago to save Mithya from the Great Crisis.

Under the watchful eye of Shuk Tee, the Emperaza's most trusted advisor, and the guidance of three expert

Achmentors—hypnotic Achalmun, who trains their minds, scatterbrained Dummaraz, who strengthens their values, and full-of-fun Twon d'Ung, who fine-tunes their bodies—the Taranauts begin to blossom into brave, strong, responsible heroes that Mithya can be proud of.

For their first challenge, the Taranauts travelled to Zvala's world of Shyn with their new friend Makky, a makara with an amazing sense of smell. After many exciting adventures, they cracked the hidden riddles and rescued the four Tarasuns of Shyn, the Emeralds.

An octoll later, the Taranauts found themselves in Lustr's brain-scrambling Mayazaal, battling flesh-eating flowers, weeping trees and hostile minimits, before they set the Sapphires free. Their new friend, Zubreymunyun, the mysterious aquauto driver with 'connections', proved to be very helpful indeed.

In Sparkl, the world they chose to tackle next, the three had to play and win four deadly games if the Amethysts were to be saved. In the end, the Taranauts' winning mix of superskills, razor-sharp intelligence, and heart, combined with superb teamwork, sees them through.

In his citadel, Xad Yantra, Shaap Azur is getting increasingly desperate. He assigns young, brash Ograzur Dusht the task of finding a traitor in Shoon Ya's camp.

Now a traitor has been found, and the Taranauts are in serious danger. Can they stay safe, and more importantly, rescue the Rubies? Now read on . . .

Mithya

Mithya A whole different universe, with eight worlds—Dazl, Glo, Shyn, Shimr, Lustr, Sparkl, Syntilla, Glytr—that bob around in the endless sea of **Dariya**, around the bad-tempered volcano Kay Laas. On top of **Kay Laas**, in the Land of Eternal Taralite, lives ShoonYa, the Emperaza of Mithya.

Tara The rainbow-coloured supersun of Mithya. Tara has 32 stars in eight iridescent colours—the Emeralds, the Sapphires, the Amethysts, the Rubies, the Silvers, the Citrines, the Turquoises, and the Corals.

Tarasuns The 32 stars that make up Tara.

Taraday A day on Mithya. It is 48 dings long.

Taralite From 1 o'ding to 32 o'ding, the Upsides of the eight worlds, where most mithyakos live, stay out of the water and enjoy the cool colourful light of the Tarasuns. This part of the Taraday is called Taralite.

Fliptime At 32 o'ding, all the worlds flip over into Dariya. The moment when this happens is called Fliptime.

Taranite From Fliptime until 48 o'ding, the Upsides are turned away from Tara and into Dariya. During this time, they are in darkness, their buildings and vehicles and forests protected with force-fields called **Dar-proofs** which prevent water from seeping in.

Downsides The halves of each world that stay in darkness, inside Dariya, for 32 dings each Taraday. These are scary, unexplored places, populated by creatures of the darkness and not-so-nice mithyakos.

Xad Yuntra The secret hideout of Shaap Azur, Emperaza Shoon Ya's evil twin.

Magmalift A magma-powered elevator inside Kay Laas in which mithyakos can zoom up to the Land of Eternal Taralite.

Aquauto An amphibious cab with the ability to travel both on water and on land.

Aqualimo A much fancier aquauto used by VIMs (Very Important Mithyakos) to get around.

Cabamba Another kind of cab—but this one travels only on land.

Magnarail A superfast train.

one

'Oooh! Looking spiffy there, Taranauts!'

The Taranauts whirled and grinned. Their favourite Achmentor, Twon d'Ung, was standing by the Magmalift they had just burst excitedly out of, looking admiringly at their All-Terrain Obverse Nanos—Zarpa's pair a shiny black and silver, Zvala's lavender with delicate golden swirls, and Tufan's busy with an edgy blast guitarele pattern. 'So what do these babies do?'

'May I tell? May I? Please, please, *please*?' begged Tufan, looking so eager that even Zvala didn't have the heart to protest. 'All yours, giz wiz!' she said graciously.

Tufan turned to Twon d'Ung, his eyes shining. '*So*-oh, we all know what regular Nanos do—they help you zip around at twice your regular speed on flat land. But with these . . . ,' he bent and brought the aglets of the laces of his shoes together.

Beep! As the aglets connected, the toe-caps morphed into blue-skinned touchscreens with a dozen blinking icons. 'Now watch this!' Tufan touched the icon that said 'Roll'. A line of wheels popped out under each shoe, converting them into instant rollerblades! Tufan touched the Retract icon. The wheels retreated.

'Now let's show her Slide!' suggested Zarpa. 'Sure. Stay back, everyone!' called Tufan, touching the 'Slide' icon. Slim smooth slats shot out from under the shoes, transforming them into gleaming skis. 'Clamp!' cried Zvala, unable to resist any longer. Quickly, before Tufan knew what was happening, she had touched the Clamp icon. Evil-looking crampon claws, perfect for getting a grip on snow and ice, leapt out of the sides and bottom of the shoes. Their sharp metal points grated against the skis.

'Zvaa-*laaa*!' yelled Tufan and Zarpa together. 'You have to retract the skis before you press anything else, you sillykoof!'

Zvala reddened. 'Oops! Sorry!' she mumbled quickly. Then she scowled. 'But you both don't need to gang up and yell at me like that either, all right?'

'Like you wouldn't have done the same if they had been *your* Nanos!' snapped back Tufan. They glared at each other. Zarpa bent down for a closer look. 'No damage done, you guys,' she said, 'Calm down.'

'You lucky, lucky mithyakins!' smiled Twon d'Ung. 'These are absolutely *the* coolest, most mastastic shoes I've ever seen in Mithya. Where did you get them from?'

'Aren't they *just?*' exulted Tufan, his irritation evaporating. 'The Marani of Sparkl got them made especially for us, as a reward for rescuing the Amethysts.'

'And we also got a durdekscope, a latlongmeter, a . . .'

'Time out,' called Twon d'Ung, glancing at her dingdial. 'I'm supposed to get you to Zum Skar in the next ten dinglings, or Ms Shuk Tee isn't going to be pleased. You can tell me all about your exciting new thingummies at our first session tomorrow. And,' she paused, looking mysterious, 'all of us here have something exciting to share with you as well!'

'Like what?' chorused the Taranauts eagerly.

'Tomorrow,' said Twon d'Ung firmly, although her eyes twinkled. 'Fall in line, please.'

'Aye, aye, Achmentor.' The Taranauts saluted smartly and fell in.

Twon d'Ung grinned. 'Quick march, then,' she said, taking her place at the head of the line. 'Left, right, left, right . . .'

'Well done, Dusht.'

It was said quietly, without much ceremony, but Ograzur Dusht, who adored the mithyaka on the black tantrite throne, felt his heart swell with gratitude. He bowed low. 'Thank you, Master,' he said, before adding reverently, 'There is no greater joy than serving you.'

Shaap Azur nodded, and turned to the rest of the Ograzurs. 'We have found our mole in the Emperaza's camp!' he announced, carefully avoiding his old Achmentor, Vak's eyes. 'Now we can always stay one step ahead of those meddling Taranauts. Mithya will be ours yet!'

'*Harharazur!*' The Ograzurs thumped their tables in approval. 'Mithya will be ours yet!'

Ograzur Vak joined the chorus—it would not do to show his disapproval too openly, especially because there was also, in his case, the question of loyalty. All those octons ago, when Shaap Azur was still at Zum Skar, he had promised him, Vak, a place in his closest circle when he came to power. Vak had laughed it away—he had no doubt that Shaap would become a Very Important Mithyaka some day, he had said, but he himself was a mere Achmentor, not a politician, and Shaap would surely find others younger, cleverer and infinitely more talented to help him when the time came.

Then, many octons after Shaap Azur and his twin Shoon Ya had graduated, they had found themselves rivals in the race to the ultimate prize—the Emperaza-ship of Mithya itself. In the end, Shoon Ya had become Emperaza, and a shattered Shaap merely Dewanaza of the Downside, but one of the first things he had done after taking over was to contact his old Achmentor and make good his long-ago promise. Vak had been deeply touched. Whatever he felt about Shaap's actions now, he could not betray that affection and trust.

'Even amongst ourselves,' Shaap Azur was speaking again, 'we will only ever refer to this . . . this secret *agent* . . . as Dro Hie: The Mole. His name—and I only say 'his' as a convenience, it could well be a 'her'—is known only to Dusht and myself.' Dusht beamed. There was a low rumble of disapproving murmurs from some of the other Ograzurs.

'It is for the best,' Shaap Azur went on firmly. 'That way, even if one of your Demazurs, or—Kay Laas forbid it!—one of *you* is captured, they will never be able to find out who Dro Hie is.' His eyes grew dark as he scanned the room. 'Whatever the oh-so-noble Upsiders may think,' his voice rose bitterly, 'there is a strong code of honour among the Downsiders, and we will never let the safety of anyone on our side be compromised!'

'Hear! Hear!' cheered the Ograzurs. 'More power to Dro Hie!'

At the far end of the table, Hidim Bi cleared her throat. 'Master, if I may...'

'Speak, Hidim Bi.'

'Dro Hie will need all the help he can get, and we can do better than sitting on our hands here in Xad Yantra. I suggest we create enough . . . um . . . *distractions* . . . in each of the eight worlds to keep the Emperaza's forces occupied, so that the Mole can work undisturbed.'

Shaap Azur stroked his chin thoughtfully. 'That is a very good idea, Hidim Bi. But,' he said firmly, locking eyes with his most difficult lieutenant, 'I don't want anybody hurt, mind, as far as possible.'

'Of course.'

'Will you lead that operation, please?'

Hidim Bi's lips twisted into a smile. The smile, instead of softening her face, made it look crueller than usual. 'It will be my *pleasure*, Master,' she said, bowing.

Two

In the Tower Room at the Palace, the Taranauts ran from one window to another, enjoying the view. In the north, the world of Shyn glowed a soft green, bathed in the light of the Emeralds. Way away in the southern sky, the Sapphires twinkled brightly, enveloping Lustr in azure light. And now, a purple haze lit up the eastern sea around Sparkl. Zarpa looked up at the Amethysts and sighed happily—the last octoll's challenges had been far tougher than the previous ones, and the Taranauts had had some very anxious moments, but it had all been worth it for this. Her home world, even if she did say so herself, looked heart-wrenchingly beautiful.

'I guess we're going to Glo next,' said Tufan, peering out of the western window. 'That corner of Mithya has some serious lighting issues, don't you think?'

Zvala grinned. 'I agree,' she said. 'Glo it is. What say, Zarpy?'

'I wish you would stop calling me that,' scowled Zarpa. 'But yes, onward to Glo, I guess. Have you realized that it is the first time we will be going to a world that none of us knows anything about? We don't even know anyone who lives there, do we?'

'Eeeeeeeeeeeeee!' shrieked Zvala, as a thought suddenly struck her.

'Woohooo!' cheered Tufan, looking equally elated.

Zarpa stared. 'What? What did I say?'

'*I* know someone who lives on Glo!' danced Zvala, barely able to contain her excitement. 'Well, *ac*-tually, I don't *know* her, but I do know *of* her, and so do about a mazillion other mithyakins—*Dana Suntana*! Eeeeeeeeee!'

'I know someone too!' said Tufan, his face aglow. 'My big brother! He has been away for octolls and octolls doing I don't know what, but his exams start in a couple of octites so he should be around. Dada's the coolest guy in the universe–*you'll* see. Wayyyyyy cooler than . . .'

'Don't say it!' said Zarpa quickly. 'Unless you want your eyes scratched out.' Her voice dropped to a menacing whisper. 'There's a Zvardula in the house!'

'Rrrrrowwwrrrr!' said Zvala fiercely, pink shimmer-polished claws at the ready.

The three of them burst out laughing.

'I really do seem to have the worst timing.' A deep, lilting voice cut through the merriment. 'I am always interrupting something fun.' The Taranauts gulped and turned around. 'Hello, Ms Shuk Tee,' they said, flushing.

Shuk Tee cleared her throat, and Zvala thought she saw the ghost of a smile flit across her lips. The Most Intelligent Being on Mithya was certainly stern, but she was never cold or mean. Unlike, for instance, that awful Achmentor Achalmun.

'Welcome back to Zum Skar, Taranauts. The Emperaza has asked me to convey his heartiest congratulations and deepest appreciation for your superb work on Sparkl.'

The Taranauts flushed some more.

'I have an important announcement to make this morning. We have a new addition to the faculty this octoll, a new Achmentor.'

The Taranauts sneaked a look at each other in sudden anticipation—a new Achmentor! This must be the 'something exciting' that Twon d'Ung had been talking about!

'Please welcome—Achmentor Aaq Vis Ling!'

A young, buff mithyaka entered the room, pushing his designer tarashades up his forehead and into his beautifully-set movie-star hairdo. A neatly trimmed moustache made an elegant thatch over his thin lips, stretched now in a condescending smile, and his olive skin glowed with health. He moved gracefully, like a jungle bekkat—or a dancer—but judging from the muscles that rippled like boasliths under his snug, expensive-looking bodysuit, he may have well been a wrestler or a bodybuilder. A sleek summoner—absolutely top-of-the-line, Tufan noted enviously—hung around his neck.

Zvala shot a quick glance at Zarpa, screwing up her nose slightly, and choked back a giggle when she saw that Zarpa was doing the same—the Achmentor reeked of something far worse than Tufan's Max deo!

'Achmentor Aaq is a genius at gizmotronics,' explained Shuk Tee. 'When we saw how well Tufan did at Lunascoot Latang'—Tufan turned red with pleasure—'and heard about the Marani of Sparkl's gifts to you, we realized that gizmotronic gadgets may prove very useful in your future missions, if you mastered them properly. So,' she indicated Aaq with an imperious sweep of her hand, 'we brought in our best.'

Aaq acknowledged the compliment with the teeniest tilt of his head, more interested in checking out his reflection in the polished surface of his summoner. Zarpa bristled with indignation—if Ms Shuk Tee had called her the 'best' at anything, she would have bowed so low that her forehead would have scraped the floor!

'Here are your dingplans,' went on Shuk Tee. 'We have had to squeeze in Gizmotronics into your already packed schedule, so brace up for a tough octoll.'

The Taranauts scanned their dingplans and groaned inwardly. The sessions with Achmentors Twon d'Ung and Dummaraz had been slashed, but they were still spending dings and dings with Achalmun. For the hazillionth time, Zvala wondered why her most hated Achmentor taught her most favourite subjects—this time, they were going to get deeper into Stellikinesis and Hovitation, and take their first baby steps into Stellipathy—the amazing technique of the mind-to-mind hook-up!

She saw that Zarpa was looking excited too, and turned her attention to Twon d'Ung's sessions—more Bel Nolo and Kalarikwon, of course, some rock climbing and rapseiling, and something called . . . um . . . Silambalati, the 'stick-based martial art of Glo'. It didn't sound fun in the least, just sweaty and scary—yuckthoo!

'Your first session is in half a ding, so you may disperse now. Don't be late!'

The Taranauts bowed and left.

'Read my lips—Giz.Mo.Tro.Nics!' exclaimed Tufan, his eyes wide, the moment they were out of the room. 'How *cool* is that! Not boring Mithbotany and Mithography and Mithmath, but . . .'

'Giz.Mo.Tro.Nics,' chanted Zarpa and Zvala. 'Yeah, yeah, we got that.'

'What!—you two *seriously* aren't looking forward to it?'

The girls shrugged. 'Whatever.'

Tufan was completely disgusted. 'Zarpa, you are the only mithyakin I know who has her own dingdial and summoner and Hummonica, but you're just not interested in how they work! And Zvala, you really *get* stuff like how a Latangun works like no other girl I know, but all *you* care about is glolights in a hazillion colours! Sometimes I wish there had been four Taranauts, and the fourth one had been a guy!'

'Well, I wouldn't worry too much if I were you,' said Zvala airily. 'Now that Mr Self-Obsessed, also known as Achmentor Aaq, is here, the two of you can bond over all the 'guy' stuff. Like taking things apart, maybe, or building digitronic whatchamacallits or . . . um . . . swapping evil-smelling, noxious-fume-emitting substances.'

Tufan looked genuinely puzzled. 'Evil-smelling substances? What are you talking about?'

'Oh, never mind,' said Zvala infuriatingly, linking arms with Zarpa. 'This is just *girl* stuff.' The two of them skipped away, giggling uncontrollably. Tufan shook his head, exasperated. Then he turned on his heel, and headed towards Zum Skar by the long route, putting as much distance as possible between himself and those two annoying sillykoofs.

Three

'You sent for me, Emperaza.'

The two mithyakos at the table—Emperaza Shoon Ya and Head of Mithsafety, Chief Sey Napati—looked up at the tall mithyaki who had just entered the room.

'Come in, Shuk Tee,' said Shoon Ya, waving her into a seat. 'I will be with you in a dingling.'

Taking his cue, Chief Sey got to his feet. 'I think we have discussed everything on the agenda, Emperaza. I will await your instructions.' He bowed slightly and left.

Shoon Ya walked over to Shuk Tee, his forehead lined with worry. 'There's trouble erupting everywhere, Shuk Tee. An uprising in the Upper Right province of Shyn over the Taratongue enforcement issue, anti-Maraza riots in Glytr, accusing him of not lobbying hard enough to have the Turquoises rescued before the other Tarasuns, demonstrations by SPASM—the Society for Prevention

of Arm-Twisting of Small Mithyakos—in Lustr about inadequate compensation for mistreatment, a fast-unto-death against mithyaka-rights violations in Dazl . . . I can't understand it . . .'

He paced up and down the room. 'It has Shaap Azur written all over it, of course,' he continued. 'This is exactly what he did—stir up trouble—before I sent him off to the Fiery Lands. But why *now*? With 20 Tarasuns still in his clutches, he holds all the cards. The Taranauts have done well—spectacularly well—so far, but surely Shaap is not already so insecure that he feels he has to go back to his old, tired tactics?' He paused, frowning. 'I can't shake off the feeling that there's something I'm missing in this picture.'

Shuk Tee remained silent. She had a fair idea what Shaap Azur was up to—all these disturbances were merely diversions, she guessed, meant to take Shoon Ya's attention off the real issue—the fact that someone in his camp had turned traitor. She had discovered this only a couple of octites ago, when she had sent Stellipathic thoughtwaves all over Mithya and had intercepted a snatch of an enemy thoughtwave from somewhere on the Downside.

But Shuk Tee was not about to share this vital bit of information yet. Shoon Ya's terse comment the last time they had met—'Between me, the Achmentors, and the Taranauts, Mithya is already in safe hands, thank you'— still rankled. She would not give her opinion unless he asked for it.

On his part, Shoon Ya had known Shuk Tee too long not to realize the reason for her silence. 'Oh, stop being so pandiheaded, Shuk Tee!' he burst out. 'I'm sorry I was short with you the other day. Now come on, snap out of it. You know my twin better than I—what is going on?'

It wasn't much of an apology, but Shuk Tee let it go—after all, this was her beloved Mithya's future at stake, and she needed to have Shoon Ya on her side. 'There is a traitor in our ranks, Emperaza,' she said. 'The disturbances are just a smokescreen, meant to keep Chief Sey's men distracted, while the traitor goes about his dirty work undisturbed. Shaap doesn't have the merest inkling that we know of this, so we have the advantage right now.'

'A traitor?' Shoon Ya looked skeptical. 'How sure are you about this?'

'If I wasn't quite sure, Emperaza, I would not have mentioned it. Of course I don't know yet who he—or she—is, but I mean to find out. No one is above suspicion, and I mean *no one*. I am assuming that I have your support on this.'

Shoon Ya hesitated. 'Of course you do,' he said slowly, 'but on certain conditions. You will work completely undercover on your investigation until you have hard evidence against someone. You will not have mithyakos taken in for questioning or proceed against them in any manner without clearing it with me first.'

Shuk Tee's eyes blazed, but she kept

her voice even as she stood up to leave. 'Of course, Emperaza.'

'It isn't that I don't trust your judgment, Shuk Tee. But these are strange times for Mithya. Everything lies in the balance, and I simply cannot risk offending those who are loyal to me. You do understand, don't you?'

Shuk Tee nodded stiffly and left, noticing that Chief Sey had left the door slightly ajar when he had exited. She made a mental note to be extra careful about such things henceforth.

As she stepped out of the Throne Room, she felt a sudden prickling at the nape of her neck. She whirled, scanning the length of the long corridor, and caught sight of a slim figure walking briskly away, her ponytail bobbing behind her.

'Achmentor Twon d'Ung!'

Twon d'Ung stopped abruptly, then turned and walked back, her face bright red. 'I had an appointment with the Emperaza at 12 o'ding,' she stuttered. 'But I saw you were with him, so I decided to come back another time.'

Shuk Tee nodded. 'My business with the Emperaza is done,' she said. 'You can see him now.'

Twon d'Ung knocked and went in. Shuk Tee stared at the closed door. The Achmentor's story was completely plausible, but the door *had* been ajar. The question was—how long had Twon d'Ung stood outside the door? And exactly how much had she heard?

Four

The Taranauts trooped out of Achmentor Achalmun's Hovitation session, exhausted and completely demoralized. Just a ding ago, they had been exulting at how much better they had got at Stellikinesis, and Achalamun had actually given them his highest two-word accolade—'Not bad'. Then they had moved to their first Hovitation practical, and everything had fallen apart again.

'I 'full-focus'ed and 'absolute-focus'ed and even '*infinite*-focus'ed,' groaned Zarpa. 'Fat lot of good that did me—my feet didn't even get a millinch off the ground.'

'Owwww, me too,' sighed Zvala, sinking to the floor and rubbing her feet between her hands. 'All I have to show for it is infinite pins and needles.'

Zarpa and Tufan walked on. 'Did you see how high above the ground Achalmun was hovitating?' Tufan's awestruck voice was saying. 'He's absolutely mastastic!'

Zvala rolled her eyes. She would never understand what Tufan saw in Achalmun. After all, it was Tufan who found Achalmun's sessions the hardest to cope with, and the Achmentor could be a real meanie to his weakest pupil. But the dum-dum just *adored* him . . .

'Utterly incomprehensible!' said a voice.

'Exactly!' agreed Zvala. Then she shot to her feet, gulping like a meenmaach. It was Achmentor Achalmun, now making his way past where she sat, who had spoken! Or had he? His face looked as expressionless as ever, and he had apparently not noticed her sitting there at all, but Zvala could have sworn it had been his voice. She froze—Stellipathy! Achalmun had read her thoughts and spoken straight into her mind! She would have to warn the others——their most private thoughts were not their own anymore——and had never been!

Achmentor Aaq waved his slim manicured fingers, each fitted with a snug sheath shimmering with neurowires, like a magician, and a rectangle of light appeared on the smooth white wall in front of him. With his index finger, he began to write in the air. As he wrote, the word 'Aaq Vis Ling, Genius' appeared on the screen. He turned around to face the Taranauts, brought his thumbs and index fingers together in a rectangle, held it away from him like he would a freezeframe, stretched his thin lips into a superior smile, and 'clicked'. Instantly, his picture joined the words on the screen. Turning towards the screen, he waggled his fingers to move the picture and the words around until he was satisfied.

'Something's missing,' he murmured. 'Ah yes, my summoner.' He 'clicked' again. Instantly, the summoner diffused into a shower of brilliant sparks. The sparks reappeared in the picture, reconstituting rapidly in Aaq's pocket until the summoner was whole again.

Burrrr! Burrrr! 'Oh-oh,' said Aaq. 'Excuse me while I get that call.' He reached into the picture and pulled out the summoner. The whole phenomenon repeated in reverse. The Taranauts gasped. 'Be back in a dingling,' called Aaq over his shoulder, 'while you digest what you have just experienced—the power of MISTRI.'

Quickly, Zvala pulled out her pocket Wikipad and typed in MISTRI. 'Molecular-level Imaging for Seamless Translocation and Reconstruction Interface,' she read. 'A cutting-edge sixth-sense technology by which material objects can move between the physical and digitronic worlds. Beta testing in progress. One octon to market. Inventor: Aaq Vis Ling.'

'Whoaa! My brain's spinning,' exclaimed Zarpa. '*What* was that again?'

'*That* was just the purest coolness!' said Tufan. 'Basically, it means that you can take any 3-D object and convert it into a 2-D picture!'

'Um,' said Zarpa. 'Dumb question, but isn't that what a freezeframe does?'

'Yes, but with MISTRI, you can also convert the 2-D picture *back into the 3-D object*!' cried Zvala.

'Exactly!' said Tufan. 'But like it says here, beta testing is in progress, which means MISTRI isn't quite perfect yet, not quite free of bugs and glitches, and it might take another octon before it is ready to package and sell.'

'Or not,' said Achmentor Aaq, flicking his hair back and checking his reflection again as he walked back in. 'The way things are going, it might be ready well before that. Nothing I make is ever far from perfect anyway.'

Zvala mentally rolled her eyes. 'How come *you* didn't disappear into the digitronic world when you took your own picture, Achmentor?'

'Ah-*ah*!' Achmentor Aaq waggled a slim forefinger at her. 'Curiosity killed the bekkat, my dear! Geniuses never tell, you know. Anyway, no one, not even the Taranauts, will get to use this revolutionary gizmology until it is good and ready, so I'm afraid,' he shrugged, 'you'll just have to hold your ashvequins till then.'

❖

'Wonder what the secrecy is all about!' frowned Zarpa that evening, when the Taranauts were horsing about with Makky and sharing the highlights of the octite with Twon d'Ung after a gruelling Silambalati session. 'Aren't Achmentors supposed to answer questions and share knowledge, Ms Twon d'Ung?'

'Of course they are!' said Twon d'Ung fiercely. 'I'm going to tell Aaq to behave himself and tell my favourite mithyakins everything they want to know. Maybe I'll kick him in the shin too, when I meet him at dinner.'

Zarpa's eyes grew round. 'You don't mean that, Ms Twon d'Ung! You'll get me into big trouble!'

'I'd say go for it, Ms Twon d'Ung!' said Zvala. 'And while you're at it, tell him to stop looking into his summoner and checking his hair every five dinglings!'

Twon d'Ung laughed. 'Aaq's okay,' she said. 'A bit of a loontoon, but absolutely brilliant. He was my junior by a couple of octons at school, and I used to bully him plenty when I was sports captain.' She paused, remembering. 'It's amazing how well he's done for himself—his family was dirt-poor, and there was tragedy too . . . His mom died when he was very young, and his little sister, who he was very fond of, went missing some octons later, so I used to look out for him . . .'

'So did *you* tell Ms Shuk Tee about him?' asked Zarpa.

Twon d'Ung stood up. 'I really shouldn't be discussing the other Achmentors with you,' she said, dusting herself off. 'But,' she winked, 'go easy on him, guys, will you?'

'Of course, Ms Twon d'Ung,' said Zarpa. Twon d'Ung waved and jogged off.

'Of *course*, Ms Twon d'Ung,' chorused Zvala and Tufan, in a perfect imitation of the mesmerized voice Zarpa always used when speaking to Twon d'Ung. Then they mounted Makky and fled, as Zarpa gave chase, screaming revenge.

Five

The octoll rolled on. The Taranauts ran about like headless kozhickens—going from one intensive session to another, slaving over assignments and making time to hone their individual superskills in between. This time, unlike before, there were a lot of frenzied goings-on at Zum Skar. Mithyakos, most of them VIMs (Very Important Mithyakos) came and went, their faces grim. All over Kay Laas, groups of mithyakos huddled over their newspapyruses, discussing the news, none of which seemed to be good, in low worried whispers.

In class, the Achmentors went through the motions, but their minds seemed to be elsewhere. Dummaraz was more distracted than usual, frequently losing his train of thought in the middle of a lesson, and arguing constantly with himself under his breath, as if the issue he had to come to a decision over was a matter of life and death. Twon d'Ung often looked worried, and stopped staying back after sessions to chat. Achalmun stayed more or less the same, but he seemed a teeny bit less demanding, a weeny bit more preoccupied. Only Aaq seemed completely unconcerned, and as self-absorbed and vain as ever.

'Have you realized,' said Zvala suddenly one evening, absently feeding Squik his zamunberries while she wrestled with one of Achalmun's ciphers, 'that we haven't seen Ms Shuk Tee at all this octoll? She used to put her head around the door quite regularly, to check on how we were doing, but it is almost the end of the octoll and . . .'

The others looked up from their assignments. 'Something's definitely up,' said Tufan. 'Of course there are all those riots and demonstrations and stuff happening everywhere, but that's not all there is to it. Everyone's jumpy, as if they are all hiding some big secret.'

'I feel it too,' agreed Zarpa. 'Uffpah! I'll be glad when this octoll is over and we're on our way to Glo. At least we will be doing something useful there, and by ourselves, away from all these nervy grown-ups.'

'Yes, and closer to Dana Suntana—hurrayyyy!' exulted Zvala. Then she stopped, looking horrified. 'Oh *noooo*—I have absolutely *nothing* to wear for the MegaStage

ceremony when we choose the next world to visit! I bet I bet I *bet* Dana will be watching the starcast, and I'm going to look like a *complete* loser—what am I going to do?' She wrung her hands, getting more and more agitated. 'Maybe I can have Ma send me all my party outfits by express delivery—do you think they will be able to deliver in two octites, Zarps? Or maybe . . .'

Beep! 1 New Message. Zarpa picked up her summoner, wondering who could be calling at this time of nite. 'It's from Ms Shuk Tee!' she exclaimed, looking at the others. She clicked the summoner on. The message was terse:

Megastage ceremony cancelled due to security concerns. Pls communicate the world you have chosen to visit next directly to me, so that arrangements can be made to get you there safely.

'Hooo-rayyyy!' Hugely relieved, Zvala pumped her fists in the air.

'Heigh-ho, heigh-ho, it's off to Glo we go,' sang Zvala, 'to meet Da-na the Sun-ta-na, heigh-ho!' She danced towards the Magmalift, her backsack jumping up and down her back.

'To meet Da-*da*, the *bigger* star, heigh-ho!' corrected Tufan. He was singing completely off-key, focusing only on trying to drown out Zvala's voice as he ran.

'Hey! We also have the Rubies to rescue,' yelled Zarpa testily. But Zvala and Tufan had already raced ahead. She ground her teeth in exasperation.

Since the news had come in, late last nite, that Dana Suntana would personally be there to welcome the Taranauts at Glo, Zvala had gone completely mad. She had tried on every party outfit she had had her mom dispatch to Kay Laas. She had played her favourite Dana Suntana album at full volume for a whole ding after bedtime. She had driven Zarpa nuts with her questions: 'Does this look better than this with this, or with this? These earrings—too showy? What glolights? Zarpaaaa, come *on*—you have to have an opinion on *some*-thing! Oh, also, what are *you* going to wear? Not those old boring stretch tees *again*, I hope.'

At that, Zarpa had thrown her warm razuvet over her head, dived under the pillow and refused to emerge until morning. She knew perfectly well what she was going to wear—her trusty old cargotrax with their hazillion pockets, one of her comfy dri-eazy stretch tees, and of course, her All-Terrain Nanos—and if Dana and Zvala didn't approve, they could go suck a limbulime.

It was going to be harder than ever, thought Zarpa to herself now, as the Magmalift sped Dariya-wards, to keep her teammates focused in Glo, but she would grit her teeth and do it. Someone had to, and as always, that someone would have to be her.

Six

'Hey-*ya* Taranauts!' The voice was nasal, singsong, and high-pitched. Zarpa and Zvala stepped out of the aqualimo onto the long pier and gawked unblinkingly at the tall, twig-thin girl who was sashaying towards them like a model down a runway, her knee-length pink-purple hair in two high panditails on either side of her head. She wore a fluorescent green quilted jacket over a gauzy tutu, and her stripey thigh-high stockings ended in black lace-up Obverses. Beaded bracelets stretched from her wrists to her elbows. Around her enormous eyes was painted a complicated pattern of dots and stars.

They were so busy staring that, at first, they did not notice the crew of starcasters and motionframers following the girl, recording her every move. All their motionframes and mycphones were labelled *Glolite SV*, Glo's official, government-owned starvision channel.

The girl shook hands with Zarpa. Then she turned to Zvala, and held her hands out. 'Face to face at last, girlfriend!' Zvala's mouth fell open—had Dana Suntana just called her *girlfriend*? 'Bub . . . bub . . . bub,' went Zvala, gulping like a meenmaach. Dana giggled. 'Awww—a true fan! You can, like, *always* tell those. And,' she looked around, 'there *is* another one of you, right? With a name that, like, starts with an S or an F or something?'

Zarpa rolled her eyes discreetly. 'Tufan,' she said, pointing, as he burst out of the aqualimo with Makky, light and happy after having just 'rained' in the shower stall.

'There you are!' squealed Dana. 'Hel-*lo*, you! And hello,' she wrinkled her pretty nose and stepped back a couple of paces, 'you big, smelly animal!'

Tufan put a protective arm around Makky. 'He is a makara,' he said, barely keeping his temper in check. 'And his name is Makky.'

'Whatever,' shrugged Dana. 'I find all animals, like, *ewwwww*!'

A merry pum-pum-para of horns cut into Tufan's angry retort. A fleet of shiny red cabambas had drawn up at the end of the pier, flags flying. One of them had the word 'Medicab' emblazoned on it, and a large white star painted on its sides. The crew of Glolite TV, which had been faithfully recording

Dana's every starry head toss, ran towards the new arrivals, mycphones extended. Dana pouted, but began to sashay back, linking arms with Zvala. Zarpa and Tufan followed, exchanging quick grins at Zvala's imitation sashay.

The back door of the first cabamba opened. Out stepped the young, stunningly beautiful Marani of Glo, her mehenna-streaked hair blowing prettily around her face. Zvala was torn. Who should she look at now—the coolest mithyateen of them all, or the Marani, who looked like a princess out of a storipad? Tufan and Zarpa did not seem to have the same problem—they just gaped open-mouthed at the elegant mithyaki in the crimson pant suit.

The Marani walked over to them in her milyard-high heels, wobbling a little as they sank at every step into the fine red sand of Glo. 'Welcome, Taranauts,' she said. 'It is such an honour to have you here. We haven't made the news of your arrival public yet,' she smiled, her ruby lips parting to reveal the neatest, whitest row of pearly teeth inside, 'or you would have been mobbed.'

Dana cleared her throat rather loudly. 'Oh, and of course,' she added hastily, 'so would Glo's biggest superstar, Dana.' Dana smiled and winked at Zvala. Zvala winked back, thrilled. Eeeeeeeeeee, the two of them had a real connection going here!

A distinguished looking mithyaka dressed in crisp whites stepped forward. 'Lt Mah Muntri,' he said, shaking hands with the Taranauts gravely. Dana waggled her fingers at him in greeting.

'My efficient, completely reliable second-in-command,' explained the Marani. 'I could not do without him, could I now, Muntri?'

Lt Muntri shuffled his feet and looked uneasy. 'You know you could, your Starness,' he mumbled. The Marani looked pleased.

'So, your Starness,' began Zarpa, pointing at the Glolite crew. 'When do you plan to starcast the news of our arrival here? When will Shaap Azur discover that we have chosen Glo and send us our first challenge?'

The Marani smiled grimly. 'You naïve mithyakins! Do you really think that Shaap Azur does not know you're here already?' Her voice dropped to a fierce whisper. 'Have you never heard of Stellipathy? He knew where you were headed the moment *you* knew!'

The Taranauts blanched.

'Well,' began Lt Muntri hesitantly, looking at the Marani for permission to speak, 'you have plenty in your favour, Taranauts. Mithyakin thoughtwaves are most unusual, and most complicated, very difficult for grown-ups to interpret. It also takes a mazillion watvolts of energy to untangle their shiny, silken strands from stronger, darker grown-up thoughtwaves.'

'Get real, Muntri,' snapped the Marani. Muntri shuffled back a few paces, looking unhappy. 'You know as well as I do that Shaap Azur and his Ograzurs have that energy—and *they will use it!*'

Zarpa swallowed, but kept her voice steady. 'If Shaap Azur already knows we are here, your Starness, has he sent any word at all about where we are supposed to begin looking for the Rubies?'

The Marani shook her head. 'Not yet. But be warned, Taranauts, you are in grave danger on Glo. Remember the Mithyamap tags at the last Megastage ceremony?'

The Taranauts looked at each other, aghast. The last octoll at Kay Laas had been so busy that the way the worlds had been tagged had completely slipped their minds. Now all the scary phrases were coming back—Endgame, Pain & Peril, Terror Trail . . . Glo had been tagged as well. 'Hostage Horror!' cried Zvala, suddenly remembering.

'Exactly,' said the Marani. 'One, or all three of you, could be abducted, kidnapped, taken hostage. We have to make sure you are protected, supervised at all times! The other mithyakos would never forgive the Glokos if anything happened to you!'

'Supervised at all times?' said Zarpa. 'By whom?'

'My first thought was to send our highly-skilled Black Bekkat commandos along,' explained the Marani. 'But the Emperaza felt that would just provoke Shaap Azur into sending his own forces out, which would result in innocent mithyakos getting hurt. To be fair to Shaap Azur, he hasn't actually ever attacked you so far, has he?'

The Taranauts looked doubtful. Images of vengeful minimits, vicious Rapacious Voracious flowers, fearsome wilderwolves, and hissing seasliths flashed across their minds. But they kept silent.

'And so,' the Marani was speaking again. 'We have come up with a more creative way to keep you under supervision. I think it's quite clever, actually.'

'May I, your Starness?' squealed Dana suddenly. She was shifting from one foot to the other in excitement. The Marani nodded, then turned and walked a few paces away to confer with Lt Muntri in private. The Glolite crew zoomed in on the superstar of Glo.

'The grand new plan!' said Dana, throwing out her arms dramatically. 'We are going to go rescue the Rubies—*together*! Isn't that, like, absolutely *mastastic*?'

Tufan goggled. '*What?!* You . . . you're . . . joining us?' He glared accusingly at Zvala—he was sure she had had something to do with it. But Zvala looked equally baffled.

'Yes, yes, and *YES*! And it's going to be so much fun! Here's how it will work. A crew from Glolite SV—these guys—will film your entire adventure as a reality show, with me as the, like, *celebrity* hostess. We're calling it '*Who wants to be a Taranaut?*' Glolite SV's ratings boom, you guys stay safe, and *I* get to host my first reality show. Many hakybirds with one stone—win win *win*!' She smiled her famous mazillion-watt smile and batted her eyelashes rapidly.

Zarpa and Tufan looked horrified. 'But . . . but . . .'

'Wo-weee!' squealed Zvala, vowing to put half a ding aside for eyelash-batting practice every single nite. 'What a brilliant idea! I *so* can see myself as a Star Vision star. And then maybe I could launch my own fashion label—just like you, Dana—and we could have Taranauts bobble-head dolls, and . . .'

'You got it, girlfriend!' Dana and Zvala giggled. 'But first,' Dana looked critically at Zarpa and Tufan, 'these two need, like, a *total* makeover—new wardrobe, cooler hair, make-up . . . I've just met this amayyyyyzing make-up guy,' she pointed to the patterns on her face. 'Like, cool, huh?'

'Absolutely!' agreed Zvala, who had been ogling Dana's face admiringly since she had first appeared. 'And I, like,' she giggled, 'totally agree that these two need a makeover . . .'

'Stop!' Zarpa was furious. 'The Taranauts are not performing monkapis! We have a job to do—and we don't need a celebrity hostess getting in the way!'

'Oh-hhh,' Dana was stunned for a dingling. Then her enormous eyes filled with tears. 'That's, like, *very* rude! Uhhh . . . my migraine!' She clutched her forehead and swayed on her feet. Two beefy young mithyakas appeared out of nowhere and carried her away to the Medicab. The starvision crew ran excitedly after them—action already!

The Marani and Lt Muntri were still deep in

conversation. They did not seem to have noticed the commotion yet. Zvala turned angrily on Zarpa. 'Did you *have* to be so rude? Seriously, Zarpa, sometimes you are just too much!!'

'Oh, hush!' hissed Zarpa. 'Are you completely out of your mind, Zvala? Didn't you hear what the Marani said? While you plan your fashion label, Shaap Azur could be planning something terrible for us! Also, there are four Rubies still missing.'

'Uffpah!' growled Zvala. 'Like you are the only one who knows the meaning of responsible! Neither Dana nor I ever said anything about abandoning the Rubies, in case you didn't notice. The whole reality show thing is just a front, to keep us safe! Or weren't you listening?'

'Yeah, right! I'm sure there will be plenty of time to plan rescues when you and that pink-haired loontoon are done preening and posing for the motionframes. Reality show, my eye! This is a serious *crisis*—not some make-believe prime-time entertainment for the mithyakos!'

'Dana Suntana is not a loontoon,' said Zvala coldly. 'She is an *amazingly* talented teen idol, a *highly* sensitive artiste. It's fine if you don't like her music, but it isn't fair to pass judgment on her as a person.'

'Oh please! Don't you see that all she is interested in is the ratings of the show? For a brainiac, you can sometimes be super dense!'

'That does it!' snapped Zvala. 'Katti!' She made the sign of zipping up her lips—she had no wish to talk to Zarpa anymore.

'Katti to you too!' retorted Zarpa, zipping up her lips securely.

'Fine!'

'Fine!'

'Whoaaaaa!' Tufan came alive. He agreed entirely with Zarpa's views, but had wisely stayed out of the proceedings until now. But this had gone too far. 'And how are we supposed to work as a team if two of the three are not talking to each other?'

'We're both still talking to you!' pointed out Zarpa, still fuming. 'So you can make yourself useful by carrying messages back and forth.'

'Ex-*cuse* me!' began Tufan indignantly. 'But . . .' He stopped suddenly, listening. 'Do you hear that?'

'I *feel* it,' said Zarpa, her face suddenly fearful, as the ground began to throb beneath their feet. 'What is it—a mithquake?'

'No—worse!' yelled Zvala, pointing. 'Look!'

Seven

'The Taranauts looked, and froze. Out of a haze of red dust kicked up by their monster wheels, a hazillion black and silver Bulletbikes were bearing down on them at zipspeed. The light of the arcalamps glinted blindingly off the riders' mirrored face-helmets, forcing the little group in the centre to squint and shade their eyes. The Marani screamed. Lt Muntri barked out orders. The royal security guards jumped out of the cabambas and got into position, forming a defensive circle around the Taranauts and the Marani, their long, smooth Silambalati sticks at the ready.

'Dana!' yelled Zvala, suddenly remembering. 'She's in the Medicab! Get her into the circle!'

But it was too late. The Bulletbikers were almost upon them now!

Screeeeech! As the royal guards swung their sticks, the bikers slammed down on their brakes, turning their bikes smoothly around in a single seamless motion. Some were not so lucky—as their bikes screeched to a halt, the riders went sailing through the air and into the circle. Others caught a swinging stick in the midriff and flew off, leaving their bikes to skidslide along the ground, wheels spinning madly, engines whining in protest.

Zarpa decided to take charge. 'Look sharp, Taranauts!' she ordered. 'Zvala, fire! Tufan, blow! Take care of the Marani! I'm going to get Dana!'

At the sound of Zarpa's calm, firm voice, Zvala and Tufan snapped into action. They were the Taranauts—they didn't need anyone to protect them! They raced away in opposite directions, giving each other a grim-lipped thumbs-up as they went. For a dingling, at the edge of the circle, they both stood still, Zvala willing her body to go quiet as she focused on the flame in the centre of her forehead, and Tufan repeating the Chant of Deep Stillness as he filled his lungs to bursting. Then they crashed through the circle and into the battlefield, ready to take on the enemy.

Peering over a royal guard's shoulder at the edge of the circle, Zarpa surveyed the chaotic scene, considering the best and quickest route to the Medicab. It would be madness to try and race *through* flying Bulletbikers and swinging Silambalatis—she would have to go *around* them. She backed up, and ducked out of the circle at the point closest to the pier. Then, locking her feet around one of the pillars that held up the pier, she began to stretch. She stretched and stretched, snaking around the edges of the action, staying safe and unobserved while getting closer and closer to the Medicab.

When she was stretched almost to the limit, she stopped for a quick glance around. The Medicab was closer now, and so far, no one seemed to have realized who was in it. She was much stronger now than she had ever been, and could stretch herself a little more quite easily, but it was still the beginning of the octoll, and it made sense to conserve her energy. The worst of the chaos was behind her—she would run the rest of the way. Quickly, she snapped back to her normal size and was just preparing to come out of her crouch when she heard them—Bulletbikes, roaring towards the Medicab! Dana had been discovered!

Zarpa leapt to her feet and began to run. She tore towards the Medicab, anxiety giving her feet wings. She was moving so fast that the bikers couldn't actually see her, but they were getting closer and closer, bearing down on her. Dana's terrified face peeked out of the back window for a dingling before she clutched her forehead and fell back. The front window was rolled down a crack, enough to let a motionframe and mycphone through. Zarpa shook her head in disbelief—what were the sillykoofs doing? They should be vamoosing, not motionframing!

'Go, go, *go*!' she yelled furiously. 'Get Dana to safety! I'll hold the bikers!'

'The driver's done a bunk!' yelled back the starcaster, his face a mask of fear. 'And I've only ever driven this thing once!'

'You never forget! That's what Papa says! Now go!'

The starcaster tumbled into the driver's seat and started the cabamba. The engine sputtered and complained, but finally caught. Zarpa whirled. The Bulletbikes were almost there. She began zigzagging furiously between the Medicab and the bikers, raising a fog of red dust that completely obscured the cabamba. The bikers hesitated, coughing and sneezing violently as the fine dust snuck its way into their noses and throats—where had this sudden whirlwind sprung from? By the time they had recovered, the cabamba was safely away.

At the pier, Zvala, Tufan and the royal guard had also done spectacularly well. When Zarpa got back there, the enemy had already begun to skedaddle, abandoning injured comrades to their fate. Sirens sounded as a fleet of Medicabs arrived to rush the wounded to the Glo Getwellateria.

'Stinking rotten mottegs!' yelled Tufan, shaking his fist at the retreating Bulletbikes. 'Get out of here and don't come back!'

'Yeah! Don't come back, you hear?' hollered Zvala and Zarpa.

'Woohoo! We did it!' cheered Tufan, as the last Bulletbike whizzed away. Then he frowned. 'Where's Dana?'

'Safe,' said Zarpa shortly, her face expressionless and turned resolutely away from Zvala's.

'Um . . . Zarpa,' Zvala said in a small voice. 'Thanks. For . . . for doing what you did for Dana. And for me.'

'I didn't do it *for* anyone,' bit off Zarpa harshly. 'I did it because it was my responsibility as a Taranaut.'

Zvala's face flamed and her eyes prickled with tears. She clenched her fists. Okay, so that was how Zarpa wanted it, was it? Alrighty then, she knew how to give as good as she got.

'Where's the Marani?'

Zvala and Tufan looked at each other in sudden alarm. They hadn't seen the Marani since they had first stepped out of the circle.

'Taranauts!' It was Lt Muntri. He looked very worried. 'Have you seen the Marani? I can't find her anywhere!'

Burrr! Burrr! 'Ah! That's probably her now,' Lt Muntri looked relieved. He pulled his summoner out of his pocket and clicked it on.

'Muntri!' The Marani sounded frightened. 'They got me! Keep the Taranauts safe— don't let them out of your sight . . . Ow!'

'Listen carefully, Lieutenant,' rasped a gravelly voice. 'Do not do anything foolish, like sending your forces after us, until you receive further instructions. If you do, you will *never* see your Marani again.'

A chilling giggle floated out of the summoner. Hostage Horror had begun.

Lt Muntri paced the floor of his office. There had been no word since that frantic summoner call—so the Taranauts still had no clue where to begin looking for the Rubies. Zarpa watched him—he seemed to have become much more confident since the Marani had disappeared, more sure of himself. The Marani of Sparkl, for whom her dad worked, was a great boss—she wondered if Muntri's boss was just a little bit of a tyrant.

'So,' Lt Muntri said finally, looking pointedly at Zarpa, 'I hear you are not comfortable with the whole reality show idea.'

Zarpa reddened. Zvala, who had spent the whole of the last evening bonding with Dana, opened her mouth to say something. Tufan stepped in smoothly, cutting her off. 'I'm sure the Marani and you meant well, Sir,' he said. 'But the Taranauts prefer to work independently. If there is some other way we could do this . . .'

'There is a way,' said Lt Muntri slowly. 'These were delivered from Kay Laas this morning.' He pulled a package out of a safe and drew out three ordinary looking summoners. 'The communications systems on Glo have of course shut down now, according to the conditions of Taratrap 8.0, but these have been programmed to transmit and receive despite the blackout.'

'If you promise to let us know where you are and send us regular updates on how things  are going,' he said, handing the summoners out, 'I promise that we will let you travel alone.'

'We promise,' said Tufan and Zarpa quickly, thoroughly relieved. Tufan examined his summoner. 'Um . . . where exactly do these transmit to, Sir?'

'To the secure summoner at the Marani's office,' said Lt Muntri. 'Oh, and also to Dana Suntana's summoner. According to the original plan, *she* was supposed to transmit your location to the secure summoner, so hers is also programmed to function through the blackout.' He shrugged. 'It's probably for the best, all things considered—hers will work as a backup for us here.'

Zvala beamed triumphantly—despite Zarpa's best efforts, she would be able to stay in touch with Dana through the octoll! Zarpa's mouth set in a grim line. There was no getting away from the Suntana girl!

'And now, if you will excuse me,' said Lt Muntri, 'there are several matters of state that require my urgent attention. You mithyakins must be tired too, so get some rest. Let me know the moment you hear something about . . . you know . . . *anything.*' He turned smartly on his heel and left.

The Taranauts slouched dispiritedly in their seats. After last evening's victory, they were raring to go—

they felt all ready to rescue the Rubies, the Marani, and anything else that needed rescuing. Sitting around doing nothing was the worst thing *ever!*

Tufan cut himself a monster slice of scrumplicious Glo by Chocolate, the national dish of Glo. He had eaten until he was stuffed at breakfast, but there was always space for Glo by Chocolate. Then he stood up and dusted the crumbs off. 'See you later, kattikoofs! I'm going to . . .'

' . . . take a shower—*we* know!' Zvala got up to leave too. 'If anyone needs me,' she added in a prim little voice to the back of Zarpa's head, 'I'm with Dana.'

Beep! All three summoners lit up simultaneously. The words *1 New Msg, Sender Unknown* blinked on the screens. The Taranauts looked at each other nervously. Then Tufan clicked on the message and began to read:

> Stars and spots spell out a clue
> The captive sighs, awaiting you
> Look closely round the oculi
> Of a pink-crested warbler, try!
> The Rubies, from the Net shall be wrung
> When the lock of the rocky cell is sprung.

It had happened—Shaap Azur had thrown them their first challenge on Glo!

Eight

Five dinglings later, the Taranauts had been joined by Lt Muntri, and, most annoyingly for Zarpa, by Dana, who had swapped her two ponytails for a hazillion tiny braids held down with shiny red tiktik clips. Lt Muntri had insisted on her being there, on account of her 'back-up' summoner.

'Well,' said Zarpa, studying the message. 'The good news is that it seems as if the rescue of the Marani and the rescue of the Rubies are connected. Notice the last two lines—the 'rocky cell' is presumably where the Marani is being held, so the lines must mean that when we free *her*, all the Rubies will be released.'

'That makes sense,' nodded Tufan. 'It also means, unfortunately, that not one Ruby will be released until the Marani is freed.' There was a dingling's silence as they digested that fact. 'Now let's get started on the other lines,' said Tufan. 'Who or what is an 'oculi'?'

'Lemme check,' said Zvala, pulling out her wikipad. 'Oculi (n),' she read. 'Plural of oculus, which means eye.'

'You—' said Tufan. 'As in Zvala?'

'No, you sillykoof—e-y-e, not I.'

'Ah okay, so we should be looking closely around the eyes of something or someone . . . .'

'Not *some*thing,' said Zarpa, looking at the riddle again. 'We should be looking around the eyes of a pink-crested warbler, whatever that is.'

'Sounds like some kind of hakibyrd,' said Zvala, keying it quickly into the wikipad. Then she shook her head. 'No results found.'

Tufan looked at Lt Muntri. 'Sir, would you know anything about the pink-crested warbler? Is it the name of some rare hakibyrd on Glo?'

Lt Muntri shook his head. 'Doesn't ring a bell, I'm afraid.'

'Or,' Zvala turned excitedly to Dana, remembering Café Feedface from their previous adventure, 'is it a popular restaurant here, or . . . or . . . a book, or . . . a *band*?'

'The *pink-skirted waddler?*' Dana screwed up her eyes, thinking hard. 'That sounds exactly like that silly batakoose Kool Karmella from Dazl, who thinks she's, like, such a *star*!' She gave a high-pitched giggle.

Zarpa turned away in disgust. 'Let's break it down. Anyone know what a warbler is?'

'To warble is to sing,' said Zvala quickly, looking resolutely at Tufan and making no eye contact with Zarpa. 'So a warbler, I'm guessing, is a songbyrd with a pink crest or crown of feathers.'

They were silent for a moment, turning it over in their heads. Then Zarpa gave a shout of laughter. 'I've got it!' she hooted. 'We've been assuming the warbler is a hakibyrd, but a warbler is actually, quite simply, anyone who sings—a singer! A singer with a pink head—remind you of someone?'

'Dana Suntana!' yelled Tufan, grinning and pointing. 'Pink-crested warbler—it seems Shaap Azur has a sense of humour!'

Only Zvala was not amused. 'Okay, so we need to look around her oculi!' she said briskly. 'Oh, oh, oh, Dana . . . that pattern around your eyes! Didn't you say you had a new make-up man who came up with it yesterday?'

'Yes, I did. I, like, *totally* hate it now, but it just doesn't come off! I've scrubbed and scrubbed!'

'Thank Kay Laas for that—that's our first clue! Can you close your eyes for a dingling?' She pulled out a scratchscribe and a papyrus pad and started copying the pattern of dots and stars.

'Awwww, this is *so* ex-*citing*!' trilled Dana. 'Fancy that! Li'l ol' me, the bearer of the first clue! Lt Muntri, do you think we can get the Glolite crew back to film just this?'

'No!' said Zarpa and Tufan together.

'Killjoys!' whined Dana. 'Never mind, I'll turn the summoner message into the title song for my next album—*The Pink-Crested Warbler*. That's, like, such a cool name!'

'So we have a pattern,' said Zarpa, studiously ignoring Dana, 'but what in Kay Laas does it mean?'

'It reminds me of something,' frowned Tufan, 'something I learnt at camp once . . . A code of some kind . . . Umm . . . . *Got it*! It's the Stelligraph code! I've forgotten what the symbols for the letters and numbers are, though—can you look it up, Zvala?'

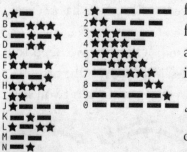

Zvala quickly keyed in 'Stelligraph Code'. The codecracker chart came up—symbols on one side, letters and numbers on the other. There was absolute silence, even from Dana, as Zvala worked on matching the pattern with the chart.

When she was done, she stared at it in puzzlement. '38 North,' she read. 'What could it mean?'

'38 North sounds like the beginning of an address,' said Tufan. 'But there is no street name or zone code.'

'It could be a latlong coordinate,' began Zarpa doubtfully.

'That's it!' squealed Zvala. '38 North, or 38N, simply means 38 degrees north of the midquator— the imaginary line that bisects each world into two semispheres! That's where we need to begin! Zarpa, you are a . . .' Then she stopped abruptly. 'Yeah,' she said to Tufan. 'That's where we need to begin.'

'You do realize,' said Lt Muntri, as the Taranauts pored over the large map of Glo he had unscrolled on his table, 'that 38N is a latlong parallel that goes *all* around Glo...'

'Yes, I was thinking about that,' said Zvala. 'Which means we really don't know exactly where to go.'

'Say again?' Dana looked completely blank.

Zarpa and Tufan also looked a little confused. 'See,' said Zvala, pulling out her scratchscribe, 'every world is divided into little squarish bits by two sets of intersecting lines. Latlong parallels slice the world up horizontally, and latlong meridians slice it up vertically. Or you could say, parallels go around each world from east to west, and meridians go from north to south. The midquator is the Main Central Parallel, which cuts the world into two equal semispheres horizontally, and the primo is the Main Central Meridian, which cuts the world into two equal semispheres vertically. With me so far?'

Zarpa and Tufan nodded.

'Like, *what??!!*' gasped Dana. 'You mean these *awful* lines are slicing and chopping my Glo into little itty-bitty pieces all the time? What keeps all the pieces together then? Favigloo?'

'They're *imaginary* lines,' said Tufan, throwing Dana a dirty look, 'that *pretend*-slice and *pretend*-chop each world. They are there to help us find places easily.' Zarpa hid a smile.

'Now,' Zvala went on hurriedly, before Dana could say anything else, 'you can find any place on the map if you know which squarish bit of the world it is located in. For that, you need its two latlong coordinates. You have to know how far north or south of the midquator the place is, and how far east or west of the primo. So if a place is at 48S(outh) and 18E(ast),

you can find its square instantly.'

'Oh, I get it!' said Zarpa. 'And our problem now is that we only have *one* latlong coordinate—38N—so we only know how far north of the midquator this place is. But we have no idea how far east or west of the primo it is.'

Tufan looked worried. 'So what do we do? Start somewhere on 38N and keep going until we come back to where we started? It's going to take several octolls to do that—and we have just one!'

'No, silly,' tittered Dana. 'You just go to the Pur Butte Peaks.' She pointed to a large mountainous area on the 38N parallel. 'Didn't the message say 'rocky cell'? So I was thinking of the music video to go with *The Pink-Crested Warbler* song and I had, like, *totally* decided to shoot it somewhere in Pur Butte—I would be the 'captive' princess and I'd be, like, all depressed and all, with my hair blowing in my face, and . . .'

'I think Dana may be right,' cut in Lt Muntri. 'Pur Butte is the only place a rocky cell *could* be on 38N. Of course,' he pointed, 'the Peaks stretch across several meridians, so you will only know where exactly to go once you have your second latlong coordinate. But this is a great start. Well done, Dana!'

'Whatever,' shrugged Dana. Tufan looked at her with new respect.

'You, like, *rock*, girlfriend!' squealed Zvala, once she had gotten over her surprise. She and Dana giggled and air-kissed like movie stars.

Zarpa gave herself a hard mental kick—why hadn't *she* thought of the 'rocky cell' part of the clue when they were looking at the map? It was so *obvious*! Now Zvala would never let her forget that it was *Dana* who had come up with the crucial bit of the answer to the riddle. Aaaaarrrrgh!

Sudden tears stung her eyes. Glo had been no fun at all so far. She hated Dana Suntana, and she missed Zvala terribly. What made it a mazillion times worse was that it was quite clear Zvala didn't miss her one teensy-weensy bit. She had found someone far more like herself than Zarpa would ever be. And now even *Tufan* thought Dana was okay. It was just not fair!

There was a discreet knock on the door. 'Someone to see Taranaut Tufan, sir.'

Tufan goggled. 'Me?' He turned to Lt Muntri. 'May I?'

'Of course,' said Lt Muntri. 'We have nothing more to discuss. I suggest all of you return to your rooms and start packing for Pur Butte.' His face clouded over. 'The path into the mountains is difficult and dangerous—even experienced mountaineers find it a challenge. Most of the terrain isn't even mapped yet, and its crags and crevasses make perfect hideouts for all kinds of desperadoes.' He paused. 'Are you *quite* sure you will be okay on your own?'

'Quite sure, sir,' said Tufan. 'We are the Taranauts.'

'Quite right,' said Lt Muntri, smiling. 'Go well, then, Taranauts.'

Tufan was out of the room first, racing down the corridor to the visitors' lounge. There was only one person on Glo who could be asking for Taranaut Tufan, and that was . . .

'Dada!' Whooping with joy, Tufan ran into his big brother's warm embrace.

Nine

Zarpa burst into the lounge next, eager despite herself to see who Tufan's visitor was. She was just in time to see the two of them disengaging hurriedly, both looking a little shocked at their own show of affection.

'So, bro?' the lanky teen, who looked exactly like Tufan would look if he had been stretched on a rack, was saying, fist-bumping the younger boy. 'How goes?'

'Oh, super, absolutely super. Killer, you know, mastastic,' Tufan's words ran into one another, and his face shone with joy, but he stayed three paces away from his brother, his hands jammed tightly into his pockets. He didn't want any embarrassing repeats of, um, you-know-what.

'You must be Zarpa,' Dada held out his hand. 'Let's see—you are the Mulkum champ, the Kalarikwon queen, the cool-headed mission leader . . . I'm sorry you have to be on the same team as this loontoon,' he pointed at Tufan. 'It can't be easy.'

Zarpa looked up into the gentle eyes, instantly charmed. Then she grinned as Dada went into elaborate, exaggerated defensive positions, trying to fend off Tufan's volley of head-butts. 'You don't know the half of it, Dada,' she said, shaking her head solemnly.

Tufan had been right, she thought—Dada *was* nice. Suddenly and fiercely, she wished she had a brother too.

'Dada?' Zvala had just sashayed into the room with Dana, and was looking expectantly at the older boy.

'Right first time, Brainiac Zvala!' said Dada. 'Like I was saying to Zarpa,' he added, in a loud aside, 'you have my sympathies for having to play on the same side as . . . Oww!' The head-butting had begun again.

Zvala giggled and turned instinctively to Zarpa, who was chuckling too. Then she quickly turned to Dana, hoping Zarpa hadn't noticed. But Dana was not giggling. She was staring at Dada, stupefied.

'And you are . . .?' said Dada, extending his hand. Zvala stared. Was it *possible* that there existed a mithyabeing who did NOT know who Dana Suntana was?

'Bub . . . bub . . . bub,' gasped Dana, her eyes bugging. 'You're . . . you're . . . Dead-Eye Darbin!'

'*Who?*' said Zvala, Zarpa and Tufan together.

'If your fortunes are dippin', and your side's getting stewed/Who d'you call but Darbin? Yeah, Dead-Eye's your dude!' chanted Dana reverentially. 'Dead-Eye Darbin, captain of the Glo-Getters, the champion Bel Nolo team of Glo. Motto—Every shot goes straight in the pot.'

'What?!' chorused the Taranauts.

'I get the Dead-Eye bit,' said Zvala, 'but where did Darbin come from?'

'Oh, I just took the letters in the name of another dead-eye, a super marksman who was reputed to never miss a shot, and scrambled it up,' winked Dada.

Tufan scowled. 'Of course I'm *always* the last to know about stuff like this, even if Dead-Eye Darbin happens to be my *own* elder brother!'

'Hey,' said Dada, mussing Tufan's hair. Tufan ducked and stomped away, still scowling. 'We haven't spoken in *octons*—I was going to tell you when I came home for the vacations.'

'Dead-Eye's, like, your *brother*?' Dana was looking at Tufan with a mixture of awe and excitement. She turned to Dada. 'Dead-Eye, Tufan's like, my *best* friend among the Taranauts.' She unlinked her arm from Zvala's and sashayed determinedly towards Tufan.

Zvala's mouth fell open. She was just beginning to feel betrayed when she caught sight of Tufan's horrified face. 'Uhhhh . . . .,' he managed finally. 'See you later, Dead-Eye!' He dashed out of the room before Dana could do the unthinkable—link her arm with his. Dana was completely unruffled.

'Umm, Dead-Eye,' she giggled. 'I have this, like, totally cool idea for a music video, where I play the beautiful captive princess. And *you*,' she pointed with one shimmer-polished fingernail—'would be, like, the *perfect* prince . . .' She giggled again, while Dead-Eye Darbin—king of the Bel Nolo field, hero of Glo, and adored big brother of Taranaut Tufan—squirmed helplessly.

Zvala glanced at Zarpa, expecting to see a cold, triumphant, 'serves-you-right' smirk. But Zarpa was looking straight at her, lips quivering, eyes dancing with merriment. Suddenly, it all seemed very funny. Zvala snorted. Zarpa snorted. Zvala hooted. Zarpa hooted. They laughed till the tears ran down their cheeks, while Dana and Dada looked on, bemused.

'Let's go, girlfriend!' said Zarpa finally. 'We have some serious catching up to do.'

'You bet! We also have a third Taranaut to find—and I think I know *exactly* where the Manic Maxphyxiator is hiding!'

They marched off to the showers, arm in arm.

'All set?' said Dada, walking into Tufan's room a couple of dings later, with Dana following close behind. The Taranauts were all there, critically examining their bulging backsacks, while Zarpa checked things off a huge list. 'So,' she was saying, 'let's go over everything one last time. One collapsible stilt-tent, three inflatable sleepsacks, retractable steelsilk ropes, clips, carabiners, and tie-offs, portable hobgaram, saucepan, frying pans, packs and packs of magginoo instachow, rain gear, heal-aids for cuts and bruises, nomopain gels for sprains and cramps, aqualeri flakes for purifying water, Born-Again Bars . . . and of course, our summoners, wikipad, latlongmeter, durdekscope . . . phew! Anything I've missed?'

'What about portalamps? And extra batteries for your hobgaram?' asked Dada.

'You don't need those when the Child of Fire is on your team, you know,' bragged Zvala. 'Light and heat guaranteed, anytime, anywhere!'

'Yes, of course!' Dada slapped his forehead, looking sheepish. He turned to Tufan. 'Oh, by the way, Tufan, here's something I dug up that's going to get you all excited—the Peaks of Pur Butte are home to a rare hakibyrd. Clue: you did a school project on it once.'

'No *way*!' Tufan's eyes grew round with excitement. 'Not . . . not the . . . Bay Runda?' Dada nodded, grinning. 'Bay Runda,' Tufan recited from memory. 'Two-headed giant hakibyrd. Habitat: upper reaches of rocky mountain ranges. Wingspan: massive—2 centillion giginches on average. Highly intelligent. Protective instincts: legendary—Bay Rundas have been involved in several mithyaka rescues through hazillions of octons. Status: severely endangered, almost extinct.' He stopped. 'Do you think we will see one, Dada?'

'Who knows?' shrugged Dada. 'Stay sharp!' He put his hands on Tufan's shoulders and pulled him closer. 'C' mere, you! Make sure you stay in touch every few dings, all right? If I don't hear from you guys for more than 24 dings, I'm going to get myself to Pur Butte, with my Glo-Getters, the Black Bekkats and anyone else who cares to come along.'

'But . . . we can't stay in touch with *you*,' said Tufan, 'we can only transmit and receive to and from the secure summoner here!'

'And who said I'm going anywhere until you all get back here safely?' smiled Dada. 'Dana and I are going to be your backup team here.' Dana waved her summoner happily. 'I came prepared to stay for the rest of the octoll.'

'You did?' chorused the Taranauts.

'I thought I was only going to see you at the *end* of the octoll,' said Tufan. 'Didn't you say you were busy with University exams?'

'Yes, I did,' agreed Dada. 'I hadn't planned to be here at all. But this morning, a strange guy turned up at my dorm. He said that Lt Muntri had sent him to get me here pronto, that I was to be part of the Taranauts backup team. And he had a letter from my Head Achmentor excusing me from my exams!' He grinned. 'I didn't need any more convincing!'

'But here's the thing,' he continued after a bit, looking puzzled. 'When I met Lt

Muntri just now, he had no idea what I was talking about! But he was happy—and a little relieved, I think—to let me help Dana with what is clearly a huge responsibility.'

Dana simpered prettily and looked adoringly at Dada.

Zvala frowned. 'It all sounds a little off, Dada,' she said. 'If Lt Muntri hadn't sent him, why did this stranger say he had? It looks as though someone was deliberately trying to get you away from the University for some reason . . .'

Zarpa shrugged. 'Well, whoever it was, I think he did us a good turn.' She threw a loaded glance in Dana's direction. 'What did he look like, anyway, this person? Did he have one eyebrow that was way-y-y above the other, like that awful Ograzur someone-or-other who wanted to referee the Bel Nolo match we played in Sparkl?'

'No-o, although this one also looked a little weird,' said Dada. 'He had this indigo-gold braid down his back, and he was driving a blue-and-silver aquauto, and he insisted on blasting LB songs all the way here . . .'

'Zub!' yelled Zarpa and Tufan, red with excitement. 'He *always* knows what to do! Where did he go?'

'Search me!' Dada spread out his arms in bewilderment. 'He just sort of . . . vanished!'

'Why am I not surprised?' said Zvala darkly. 'That Zub's always up to something—and I'm not sure it's all good . . .'

'Oh, quit it, Zvala,' said Tufan. 'If Zub's around, we have nothing to worry about. What's more, Dada is

totally going to be in charge of things here, so . . .,' Dada shot him a look, 'and, oh yeah, so will . . . uhhh . . . *Dana*, so we are in really good hands.'

'Awwww,' Dana clutched her hands together and smiled at Tufan, 'you're sweet.' Tufan shuddered.

'Time to be off, then,' said Zarpa. 'Who's the team with the big, big dream?'

'*You* a-a-are, you are!' cheered Dada.

'Take care of Makky for me, Dada!' Tufan threw his arms around the makara, who had come to see them off. Dada put his hand over his heart. 'I promise!'

'Remember my music video!' called Dana, as the Taranauts piled into the cabamba. 'Do some location-hunting for me while you're there! Someplace where the rocks have, like, leeetle pinky streaks, to match my hair, would be *purrrfect* . . .'

Ten

Zvala heaved her heavy backsack out of the cabamba and stared at the forbidding panorama before her. To her right and left, as far as the eye could see, stretched the Pur Butte range, grim and grey, its contours made more sinister by the weak light of the faraway Tarasuns. Out of the ground rose sheer walls of rock, reaching for the sky with craggy fingers. Along their tops marched a jagged line of sawtooth peaks, shredding the thick fog that blanketed them into untidy white ribbons. Caves and crevices, gouged out by the elements over a mazillion octons, pockmarked the steep rock faces, giving Pur Butte countless eyes to spy with. Zvala shivered—it was all breathtakingly beautiful, in a very scary kind of way.

'Yo!' Tufan punched her shoulder. 'Scared?'

'Me?' bristled Zvala. 'No *way*! Let's go!' She started walking briskly forward.

'Whoaaaa!' Tufan pulled her back hard. 'If you will first *look* where you're going, Taranaut Zvala!'

Zvala looked. She had been so wrapped up in the misty heights of Pur Butte that she hadn't noticed that the ground fell off steeply just a few metrinches ahead of her. She walked carefully to the edge and peered down. A sluggish river of viscous black mud boiled and bubbled evilly at the bottom of a deep gully, steam rising from it in damp, scalding clouds. Zvala stepped back hurriedly, shuddering.

'Yeah, let's take this slowly,' Zarpa tossed an imlichi bubblechew into her mouth, clicked on her latlongmeter. 'We're at 38N and 18W,' she read. 'That's the 18th meridian west of the primo. There is a bridge at 20W, two meridians over. And we're standing at the edge of . . . the Budbudana River—oops!' The bubblechew wrapper slipped from her grasp and fell towards the boiling river. Instantly, with a loud sucking noise, a geyser of hot mud shot up towards the wrapper, swallowing it with a sickening squelch.

'And that,' Zarpa's voice was suddenly small and flat, 'is what will happen to anything that falls in it.'

'Okay,' said Tufan briskly, trying to sound braver than he felt. 'Let's get to the bridge then. I'm sure it is pretty safe—Glokos must use it *all* the time. Zarpa, send off a message to Dada, will you?'

Beep! 1 New Msg—Taranauts.

Dada shot out of his seat and crossed the room to Dana in three quick paces. 'At Pur Butte. Heading 2 bridge. Will msg when . . . aX—aX?' read Dana. 'Oh, I guess they mean a-*cross*, not aX. Those Taranauts— they're, like, *scary* smart.' She messaged back. 'Miss u already!'

Beep! 1 New Msg—Undisclosed Sender.

Ograzur Dusht clicked on his summoner. 'At Pur Butte. Heading 2 bridge. Will msg when across,' he read, his face twisting into an approving smile. 'Well done, Dro Hie.' Quickly, he called his trusted Demazur at Pur Butte. 'The brats are getting to the bridge. You know what to do.'

'There's the bridge!' yelled Zvala, half a ding later, pointing to where a sturdy-looking cable bridge swung slowly over the Budbudana River. Then she froze. 'Uh-oh, reception committee!'

Three mean- looking mithyakas on mangy wilderwolves were trotting slowly up to the other end of the bridge. One of them held up a scroll. 'You took your time

getting here, brats!' he hollered. 'Here's your second riddle—come and get it!'

'You bet we will!' yelled back Tufan. 'Come, girls!'

'Tufan, wait!' Zvala's voice had a frantic edge to it. 'It might be a trick!'

Tufan hesitated.

'What's the matter?' taunted the Downsider. 'Hanging around with girlkins making you go soft?'

Tufan flushed. He was *not* soft! He might 'hang around' with girls, but he was also the brother of Dead-Eye Darbin. He started walking firmly towards the bridge.

'Tufan, don't be a sillykoof! They're simply trying to provoke you!' warned Zarpa. 'Stay here until I take a closer look at the bridge with my durdekscope!'

But Tufan was running now, racing along in his Obverse Nanos, wilfully shutting Zarpa out, intent only on proving just how tough he was by getting across the bridge.

Zarpa put her durdekscope to her eyes and scanned the cables from which the bridge swung. Then she went white, and passed the 'scope mutely to Zvala. Zvala raised the 'scope to her eyes, zoomed in on the cables, and gasped—several of the cables had been hacked away at, leaving the bridge suspended by mere threads! 'Tufaaaaaan!' yelled the girls, running towards the bridge. 'Come baaaaack!'

Over his shoulder, Tufan saw Zarpa and Zvala gaining on him. He couldn't let them stop him, he couldn't! He ran faster and faster—there! He had gained the bridge now! He covered the last few metrinches in a

flying Kalarikwon leap, and landed on the bridge with a triumphant thump. The bridge groaned.

SCREEEEEECH!

With a great flapping of giant wings, an iridescent blue-green hakibyrd swooped out of the sky and zoomed across the bridge, its two enormous heads making straight for Tufan. In its talons, it held a large boulder threateningly. Tufan yelled in fright, then turned and fled.

The moment Tufan was safely off the bridge, the hakibyrd shot skywards. Then it let go of the boulder. The boulder landed in the exact centre of the bridge with a sickening crash. Screeching and wheeling, the hakibyrd rose and headed off to the rocky heights it had come from.

For a moment, nothing happened. Then, suddenly, one of the cables holding up the bridge gave, with a deafening SNAP! It was louder than any patakracker Zvala had ever heard. The bridge shuddered.

SNAP! SNAP! SNAP! Cables were splitting all along the bridge's length! The bridge hung precariously in midair for a dingling, then plunged towards the ravenous river. Tufan watched, shell-shocked, as geysers popped up everywhere, sucking greedily at every bit of bridge they could find until they had devoured it completely.

'Shame on you, you cowardy creposas!' Zarpa shook her fists angrily at the trio. 'Next time, fight fair!'

The trio only guffawed. 'Well, it would have been a treat

 to see you three go down as well, but no matter,' called one of them. 'You are still on that side, and your riddle,' he brandished the scroll, 'is on *this* side. Have a good Taraday, brats, and may the Marani rot forever in her cell.' He tossed the scroll to the side of the path and rode away with his companions.

'Hey, big-macho-guy-type person!' Zvala put an arm around Tufan, who was shivering uncontrollably. 'Everything's fine now.' Tufan sneaked a quick glance at her—no, she wasn't being sarcastic. He relaxed. 'Sorry, guys,' he said, rubbing his forehead ruefully. 'I was being a little silly there.'

'Thank Kay Laas for the Bay Runda and his protective instincts,' breathed Zarpa. 'He just came out of . . . nowhere!'

'She,' corrected Tufan. 'Only the female has that distinctive blue-green colouring. And as you can imagine, her protective instincts are far more developed than the male's.' He was silent for a moment, remembering. Then he looked around, his eyes shining, as a thought suddenly struck him. 'Maaaaaaan! Has it even sunk in yet? We saw a *Bay Runda*, a real, live Bay Runda! Do you girls even realize how lucky you are?'

'Well, she was certainly lucky for *you*, Mr Sillykoof!' said Zvala sternly.

'Yeah, well,' Tufan quickly changed the subject, reddening. 'We still have to figure out a way to get to the other side, you know.'

'Easy-peasy!' said Zarpa. 'I clip a retractable rope to my waist, then lock it and my feet around something on this side, and s-t-r-e-t-c-h across the river until I find something to hold on to. Then I secure the rope to that something, and you both get across using the rope.'

'Don't be an absolute dum-dum,' scolded Zvala. 'Even if you *can* stretch as far as the other side, which I doubt, you will be so thin and light by then that you might just flop river-wards, and you know what will happen then.'

'But that will *not* happen,' said Tufan slowly, 'if I keep a constant flow of air going under Zarpa, a current that she can 'ride'. It will make sure that she never flops downwards, *even* if she doesn't make it all the way to the other side on her first attempt.'

An arcalamp lit up inside Zvala's head. 'You know what would make it even more foolproof? A cape! Then Zarpa would have 'wings', like a hakibyrd, and she can, like, *totally* fly!'

'Yeah, *totally*,' mimicked Tufan. 'Looks like someone's just had an attack of Dana Suntan-itis.'

77

Zvala stuck her tongue out at Tufan and rooted around in her backsack for something that could serve as a cape. 'My warm cuddlewool poncho!' she squealed, pulling out a soft white poncho with pink teddy baloodis embroidered all over it. 'It's perfect!'

Zarpa slid the poncho over her neck. 'Awww!' said Zvala. 'You look so cute in it—you should wear stuff like this more!' Zarpa grimaced and rolled her eyes skywards. 'The things a Taranaut has to do!'

Quickly, she brought out a jumbo coil of retractable steelsilk rope and pressed on the button in the centre of the case. The rope shot out of the case. Clipping the case to one of the carabiners hanging from her waist, she

tossed the rope around a tree nearby. The rope wound itself around the trunk and stayed fast.

Hooking her feet around the tree, Zarpa focused hard at a spreading pipalfig tree on the other side. Then she sent up a silent prayer to Shay Sha, and, keeping her eyes resolutely averted from the boiling black mud of Budbudana, began to stretch.

'Spread your arms, Zarpa!' instructed Zvala. 'But not so much that they are perpendicular to your body. Yeah, that's about right. Tufan, start blowing!'

Zarpa hovered for a dingling at the edge of the canyon. Then she gathered all her energy, and buoyed by the air current below her, lunged strongly for the other side—

and missed! If it hadn't been for Tufan, this would have been the point at which she would have become a yummy snack for Budbudana's greedy geysers! She shuddered.

Tufan kept blowing. Zarpa hovered in midair, enjoying the feeling of flying like a hakibyrd. Then she took a deep breath, braced herself and lunged again over the shorter distance. Made it! Holding on to the pipalfig with both hands, she snapped back to her usual size. Then she unclipped the case from around her waist, and threw it around the tree. More rope uncoiled from the case, wound itself around the tree once, and stayed, taut and stretched.

'Okay, come on now, you two!' she called.

On the other side, Tufan and Zvala were already strapped into their harnesses. Tufan clipped his tie-off to the steelsilk rope. The other end of the tie-off dangled off the rope, ready to be clipped into his harness.

'I'm off!' he announced to Zvala. 'You've got your tie-off with you, right?'

Zvala didn't respond.

'Zvalaaa,' Tufan whirled around, exasperated. 'I said, you've got your . . .' Then he saw her white face and stopped—Zvala was plainly terrified.

'It's easy!' he said encouragingly, making his voice bright and cheery. 'We've done this a hazillion times with Twon d'Ung last octoll, don't you remember?'

'Yes,' said Zvala in a small voice, 'but that wasn't over the Budbudana River.'

'But there's no way you can fall!' Tufan assured her. 'You are strapped in, clipped on and completely safe!'

Zvala still looked doubtful. Tufan relented. 'Tell you what, you go first. Clip yourself on, and I'll *blow* you to the other side before you blink. How's that?'

Zvala cheered up. 'Now you're talking, Windchild!' she said gratefully. 'Sometimes, even *you* can be not quite brain-dead!'

'All right, All right,' snapped Tufan. 'Now go already!'

Zvala clipped her harness onto the tie-off, pulled herself up and wrapped her feet around the rope.

Tufan filled his lungs to bursting. Then he stood a little behind Zvala, and let it all go in one ginormous *Hoooooo!*

'Wheeeee!' Zvala squealed with delight as she slid across Budbudana at zipspeed. Two dinglings later, Tufan had joined the girls on the other side of the river.

Zarpa pressed the button on the rope case. Instantly, the rope unwound itself from the tree on the other side, and flew across the river, coiling rapidly back into the case.

'Now where's that scroll?'

'There!' yelled Zarpa, pouncing on it.

Eleven

'The Taranauts stared down at the scroll, frowning.

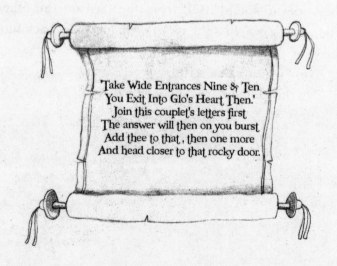

'Take Wide Entrances Nine & Ten
You Exit Into Glo's Heart Then.'
Join this couplet's letters first
The answer will then on you burst
Add thee to that , then one more
And head closer to that rocky door.

'What wide entrances?' said Tufan, looking around. 'I don't see anything here.'

'Me neither,' said Zarpa. 'Maybe the next four lines will tell us where they are.'

'The 'couplet' is obviously the first two lines of the poem,' said Zvala. 'So if we join the couplet's letters like it says here, we get . . . takewideentrancesnineandten, which makes no sense whatsoever.'

'The last two lines say to do something else,' said Zarpa. '— add thee to that . . .'

'What's a thee?' said Tufan.

'Not *a* thee, just thee,' said Zarpa. 'Thee is an old word for 'you'—right, Zvala?'

'Yup,' agreed Zvala. 'So add 'you' to something, and then another 'you' . . .'

'Youyou? Twoyou? A double you?' frowned Zarpa.

'That's it, genius—W!' cried Tufan. 'Part of our second latlong coordinate! Thank Kay Laas it is a W and not an E—it means we are already on the right side of the primo. We only need to figure out which meridian. Back to the couplet, team!'

They bent their heads over the scroll again. 'But there are no numbers here,' complained Tufan. 'There are just words—we need a *number* to complete the coordinate . . .'

'Yeah, just words, and for some reason all the words in the couplet begin with capital letters.'

'That's probably just to make sure the couplet stands out,' shrugged Tufan.

'Or *not*,' said Zvala slowly, reading the couplet again. 'You know, sometimes, in poetry, words are placed differently from prose. Like, the poem may say 'the mountain grey' or 'the magnarail swift', when it actually means 'the grey mountain' or 'the swift magnarail'. So-*oh*, here, 'Join this couplet's letters first' might just mean . . . 'Join this couplet's first letters' . . .'

Zarpa stared at the scroll. Then she looked up, her eyes shining. 'You've got it! That's *exactly* what it means! *That's* why all the first letters are capital letters! Join them, and you have 'T-W-E-N-T-Y-E-I-G-H-T—28!'

'Woohoo!' exulted Tufan. '28W, here we come!'

'You bet!' cried Zarpa and Zvala, high-fiving each other as they hoisted their backsacks onto their

shoulders. *'We'll crack each clue, till we rescue, each glo-o-owing star!'*

Beep! 1 New Msg—Taranauts.

Ridl 2 crackd. On2 28W. Bay Runda sighted—wow!!!!

Dada smiled and passed the summoner back to Dana. On the face of it, all seemed well, but he could help feeling a constant, niggling sense of concern. Surely Shaap Azur and his Demazurs had set up all kinds of roadblocks for the Taranauts! He wondered what lay between the lines of the short, cheery messages—how much were Tufan and his team keeping to themselves?

'I'm going to find Lt Muntri and let him know,' he said. 'Coming?'

'You go on, Dead-Eye,' said Dana. She giggled and whispered, 'I need the little girls' room!'

'See you later, then,' Dada waved and walked off.

Ten dinglings later, Lt Muntri walked into the Marani's office. Dana was sitting there, twirling her pink ponytails between her fingers and lip-syncing to her latest hit as it played into her head from her Hummonica.

'Oh, hello there!' The Lieutenant was a little taken aback. 'What are you doing here?'

'Dead-Eye went off to look for you, and I guessed the two of you would eventually land up here,' shrugged Dana simply, still moving to the song.

Muntri frowned. 'Why was Dead-Eye looking for me?' he asked.

'There was a new message on my summoner.'

Lt Muntri clicked on the secure summoner in the office. *No New Msgs*. His brow furrowed.

'May I come in, Sir?'

Lt Muntri waved Dada in. 'Dana said she just had a new message,' he said, looking puzzled. 'But it hasn't been received here.'

Idly, he clicked on the inbox, and opened the last message received.

Ridl 2 crackd. On2 28W. Bay
Runda sighted—wow!!!!

Lt Muntri sat up, startled. 'Well, I'll be!' he sputtered. 'The message *has* been received, after all! Only, someone else opened it first! That is why it isn't showing up as a new message anymore!' He paused, looking baffled. 'How is that possible, though? Only the Marani and I know the password.' He glowered at Dana, suddenly suspicious.

'Not only has someone opened it,' Dada spoke through clenched teeth as he scrolled through the inbox, 'but someone has also *sent it forward!* And it isn't just this message—the last one has been forwarded too!'

'Forwarded?' exclaimed Lt Muntri. 'To whom?'

'Can't tell,' shrugged Dada. 'It just says *Undisclosed Recipient.*'

Lt Muntri strode to the door. 'I want the Chief of Glosafety in here—*now*!'

The Chief arrived soon after, a little out of breath. 'There has been a severe breach of security in the Marani's office,' barked the Lieutenant. 'From this dingling on, homeland security threat levels stand upped to High Alert—Code Orange. This door,' he pointed, 'is to be kept locked at all times, 48/8, until the Taranauts return. No one, not even you or I, should be allowed to enter alone. If someone needs to enter, you or I should always be present with them. This summoner,' he held it up, 'will be locked away in this safe, and the safe's iris scanner will only recognize your iris pattern and mine. Is. That. Understood?'

'Yes, Sir. Effective immediately.' The Chief of Glosafety hurried away.

Lt Muntri looked at Dada. 'We've got it under control now,' he declared confidently. 'It won't happen again.' Dada nodded grimly. Try as he might, though, he could not push away a chilling thought—had the security measures come too late to help the Taranauts?

Beep! 1 New Msg—Undisclosed Sender.

'That interfering Bay Runda!' spat Dusht, as he read out the message to the assembled Ograzurs. 'But Paapi's teaching her a lesson she'll never forget!'

Raaksh shrugged philosophically. 'Forces of nature, Dusht!' he said. 'There are some things that even *we* cannot control. Luckily for us, though, there are plenty of things we can.' He chuckled. 'Like 28 W, for instance—the brats will never crack that one.'

All the Ograzurs, save one, snickered. 'I think we are all forgetting that they are only mithyakins, those three,' said Ograzur Vak quietly. 'Extraordinarily courageous, of course, and very gifted, but still mithyakins. It isn't right to treat them like we would enemy soldiers . . .'

'You're losing your mind, you old fool,' Hidim Bi's voice was pure venom. 'Shoon Ya is the enemy, and the Taranauts are his soldiers. Get it? If you don't agree, maybe you don't belong here.'

'He never did, Hidim Bi,' hissed Shurpa. She looked daggers at Vak. 'There is talk on the streets of the Downsides, Ograzur Vak. They are saying that in your heart, you have always loved the other one more. But your precious ShoonYa didn't think of you, did he, when he became Emperaza?'

Ograzur Vak stood up. 'The opinions of others can be fascinating, I'm sure,' he said with dignity, 'but I've always kept my own counsel. Good day, Ograzurs.'

The Ograzurs watched him go, wishing he would never come back—the old mithyaka had an infuriating way of making them feel small and mean.

Twelve

'28W—ouch!' Zarpa's voice had a worried edge to it. She was poring over her latlongmeter, dangling her feet in the cold mountain stream beside which the Taranauts had pitched their stilt-tent the night before.

'What is it?' mumbled Tufan through a mouthful of utterly satisfying leftover magginoo instachow. Zvala, on wash-up duty this morning, looked up, equally curious.

'The terrain around 28W looks really scary,' replied Zarpa. 'Tiny paths cut into the sides of steep cliffs, plenty of loose gravel everywhere . . .'

'Pshaw!' dismissed Tufan. 'Worry not, Ms Zarpa!' Pulling his All-Terrains towards him, he put the aglets of the laces together, and touched the 'Grip' icon. Instantly, strips of the thick sole retracted, creating a pattern of alternating deep indentations and raised bits. 'See—a good and proper lug sole!' he declared. 'Perfect for traction on loose gravel!'

Zarpa brightened somewhat. 'All right, then,' she said, getting up and stretching. 'Time to be off—we achieved very little yesterday, and now we are already on octite 6 of the octoll. We just have to have to *have* to make it to 28W today or we'll never rescue the Marani in time.'

'Not our fault,' retorted Zvala, clambering up the rope ladder into the tent, clean dishes in hand. 'Who knows where that sudden landslide came from? I bet it was Shaap Azur's goons who sweetly organized it, just so that we could walk an extra twenty milyards!'

Rolling up their sleepsacks and packing quickly, the girls set off, their pockets bulging with Born-Again Bars and karrypaks of fortified vigorshakes, leaving Tufan to collapse the tent into a napkin-sized square and stuff it on top of everything else in his backsack. He hurried to catch up with them.

'Zvala, can you give us some light?' called Zarpa, as she stumbled along the path. 'This no-Taralite business is beginning to really depress me. And there are hardly any arcalamps here on Pur Butte.'

Zvala's limbs ached from the long trek of the previous day. Just now, she simply did not have the energy to fire herself up—she would *never* be as fit as the other two, she thought glumly. But she did not protest—the darkness was getting to her too. She began to glow bright and red, spreading a cheery glow for milyards around. Instantly, they all felt much better.

'Are we there yet?' It was a full five dings later, and Zvala was exhausted. 'I demand a long snack break!' agreed Tufan, who was bringing up the rear. 'My stomach's beginning to protest rather loudly.'

'Almost there!' yelled back Zarpa from further down the path. 'Let's not stop now—the tricky bit is just beginning. We'll set up camp on the other side of the cliff path—*that's* 28 W on my latlongmeter. It looks pretty flat and sheltered there. Come along quick—shouldn't take us more than a ding.'

'All right, then,' groaned Tufan and Zvala as they joined Zarpa. 'One ding, and not a dingling more.'

At the beginning of the cliff path, their Nanos set to Grip, the Taranauts took stock. Ahead of them, the track narrowed suddenly—they would have to walk in a single file. On the right, the path dropped off sharply into a deep ravine, whose sides bristled with black tantrite rock-shards, sharpened to glistening points. To the left, the cliffs rose steeply, their sides oddly smooth, as if someone, determined that no climber should find purchase on it, had neatly filed off every single toehold and fingerhold.

Zarpa took a deep breath. Out came the rope. Clipping the case to her waist, she tossed the rope to her teammates, who clipped it to their own waists before slinging it around a protruding shelf of rock behind them. Tufan pulled on the rope, testing it. 'We're set.'

'Let's go. Stay safe, you guys.'

Millinch by millinch, the Taranauts crept sideways along the treacherous path, their backs flat against the smooth cliff-face. Ever so often, their shoes skidslid over patches of gravel, sending their hearts leaping into their mouths. Once, they thought they heard voices somewhere above them, and froze, too terrified even to look up and check. They spoke only when it was strictly necessary, in low, hurried whispers. Cold sweat ran in rivulets down their backs and legs, turning their palms clammy. Three-quarters of a ding later, the end of the path was nowhere in sight.

'I can't keep the glow going for much longer,' whispered Zvala, her mouth dry with fear and fatigue.

'You *have* to,' Zarpa begged, frantic. 'We can*not* do this in the dark! We're *almost* there, Zvala, once we round this corner . . .'

'Lesson for next time,' hissed Tufan, trying to lighten the mood. 'Pack the portalamps!'

'If there *is* a next time,' said Zvala hopelessly, her glow beginning to dim.

Zarpa and Tufan exchanged glances. They couldn't have Zvala lose her spirit now—they simply couldn't!

'Stop!' commanded Tufan. He closed his eyes and began to chant. 'Aaaaaa . . . uuuuuuu . . . mmmmm.'

'Aaaaa . . . uuuuu. . . mmmmmm,' repeated Zarpa, her voice a little shaky.

'Thanks, guys,' whispered Zvala. 'I know you're trying, but . . .' She closed her eyes, looking close to collapse.

'How much further?' mouthed Tufan silently to Zarpa, as Zvala's glow dimmed further.

Zarpa shrugged, and pointed down the path, where it curved around the cliff. 'I'll know once we get there,' she mouthed back.

SCREEEEECH!

The Taranauts jumped, even Zvala. The Bay Runda! She had come back to help them! They scanned the skies, but no giant hakibyrd came swooping out of it. They strained their ears for the unforgettable flapping of great blue-green wings—nothing.

SCREEEEECH! There it was again, more desperate this time.

'She's hurt!' cried Tufan. 'That's a cry of pain! And she's scared. We should go to her!'

SCREEEEEECH!

'It's coming from around the corner. Go, Zarpa, go, quickly, quickly!' Tufan's voice was harsh.

'I'm going, I'm going,' Zarpa choked back a sob, torn between wanting to go to the Bay Runda and trying to stay safe. She shuffled along as quickly as she could, Tufan urging Zvala along from behind.

'There she is!' yelled Tufan as they rounded the corner. Zvala sank to the ground. The Bay Runda was perched on a narrow rocky ledge below them, her wings folded at an odd angle.

'Oh the poor, poor thing!' cried Zarpa. 'She has broken her wings!'

'There is another possibility, brats—someone broke them *for* her!'

Tufan's head came up like a shot. A couple of milyards down, the path widened again, onto a vast flat meadow—28W! There, perched atop her handsome, snarling, silver wilderwolf, was a female Ograzur, her shaven pate shining dully in the distant light of the Tarasuns. A cruel smirk sliced her face in half.

'Why?' demanded Tufan, a cold fury washing over him. 'Because she ruined your monstrous plans at the Budbudana bridge?'

'Too right,' spat the Ograzur. 'No one, not even a Bay Runda, is allowed to mess with the Master's plans!'

Tufan turned away, shaking with anger. 'I'll stay here with the Bay Runda,' he told Zarpa, pulling out Born-Again Bars and nomopain gels from his backsack. 'You girls carry on ahead to 28W and find the third riddle.' Lying on his stomach, he leaned over the lip of the ravine to examine the wounded hakibyrd. 'The damage isn't permanent, thank Kay Laas,' he announced at last. 'And Bay Rundas heal easily. Now hurry—we're running out of time!'

★ 94 ★

SCREEEEEECH! The Bay Runda thrashed about, shooing Tufan away.

'What is it, girl?' Tufan frowned. 'What do you want me to do? You are still scared about something, right?'

'Tufan!' called Zarpa from down the path. 'The Bay Runda's nest is here, right in the middle of the path, and there are three giant eggs inside!'

'So *that's* what she is so worried about!' Tufan exclaimed. 'Bay Runda eggs need constant warmth, or they will die! And the poor thing's stuck here, unable to get to them—oh *no*, what are we going to do?'

The mithyaki on the wilderwolf roared with laughter. 'Idiot mithyakins! The dingdial is ticking away, and you waste time worrying about useless hakibyrds and their stupid eggs instead of doing what you were sent to do——rescue the Rubies!' She waved a scroll at them——the third riddle—— before hurling it from her. It flew in a wide, long arc before it hit the grass a great distance away. Then she raised her face to the sky. 'You made a poor choice of soldiers, Emperaza!' Still guffawing, she reined in her wilderwolf and rode off.

'She's right, Tufan,' said Zarpa in a small voice. 'I know how you feel, and I feel terrible too, but we have to think about Mithya now—we really should carry on. Zvala is already exhausted, and *we* can't do anything about the eggs anyway . . . .'

'*Of course we can!*' Zarpa whirled. Zvala was standing up, eyes blazing with rage at the Ograzur's cruelty. There was no fear in her anymore, no tiredness. Her anger had fired her with a new energy—she was now glowing as bright as a hazillion arcalamps. 'The Child of Fire is on your team, Captain Zarpa. Light and heat guaranteed anytime, anywhere, remember?'

As Tufan watched, open-mouthed, Zvala peeled herself away from the smooth cliff-face and walked, upright and unafraid, down the centre of the narrow path to the nest. She lay down in the nest, curling her body carefully around the eggs and stretching her arms and legs over them, warming them with a gentle heat.

'Your babies are okay, girl,' crooned Tufan. 'Zvala's taking care of them.' The Bay Runda seemed to understand. It relaxed, allowing Tufan to minister to its injuries.

'Stay put, then, Taranauts,' Zarpa's voice was tight with emotion. 'For as *long* as it takes—that's an order!' She unclipped the rope case and tossed it to Tufan. 'And wish me luck—I'm going after the third riddle alone.'

Thirteen

Standing in the middle of the immense meadow the next morning, Zarpa wondered how she was ever going to find the scroll. She had thought she knew somewhat where it had fallen, but by the time she had gotten to 28W the evening before, she had completely lost her sense of orientation. She had also been exhausted. So she had guzzled an aamberry vigorshake, finished half a brainchow bar, and hit the sleepsack, hoping guiltily that Tufan and Zvala had eaten as well.

Now, she was well-rested and ready to go, but without Zvala's light to see by or Tufan's typhoons to send objects flying into the air, she still had a task on her hands. 'Think, Captain, think!' she urged herself. If only she had someone else to help her, she thought, someone who had a particular talent for finding things that lay close to the ground, someone like . . . like . . . a *seaslith*. But seasliths did not live in the mountains . . . Ho*wever*, their cousins did! It was worth a try.

She lay down on her stomach, spread-eagled in the tall grass. 'Brotherssss,' she lisped urgently. 'Come to me, brotherssss.' She closed her eyes and thought of Shay Sha, willing him to hear her, to send help.

Well before she heard their sibilant voices or caught sight of their rough, scaly bodies, Zarpa felt her cousins check in as the ground began to thrum gently beneath her. She raised her head, her heart lifting at the sight of the rocksliths gathered around her, hazillions of them. 'Help me,' she said simply. 'Ssssearch for the ssscroll.'

The rocksliths slithered away in different directions, zigzagging across the meadow, covering every millinch of it. In no time at all, it seemed to Zarpa, one of them was zipping back towards her, the scroll clutched tightly in his mouth. Zarpa was elated. 'Thank you, brotherssss!' she said, blowing all of them kisses. 'You guyssss are the most mastastic brotherssss *ever*!'

Quickly, she unrolled the scroll and began to read.

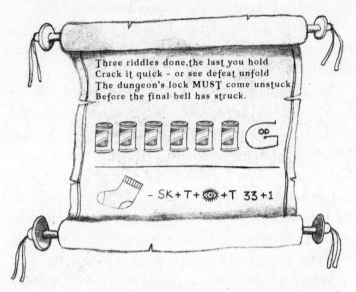

Three riddles done, the last you hold
Crack it quick - or see defeat unfold
The dungeon's lock MUST come unstuck
Before the final bell has struck.

Zarpa stared. Surely there was some mistake—this could not be the last riddle! Had the Ograzur delivered the wrong one? It seemed unlikely. Had they missed the third riddle on the way, then? Maybe things would become clearer once she had cracked this one. She pulled out a papyrus pad and a scratchscribe.

Half a ding later, Zarpa hadn't got any closer to solving the riddle. Aaaaarghh! Things were so much easier with Zvala and Tufan around! She turned a few cartwheels in the grass to clear her mind. Then she looked at the picture again.

Six boxes in a row. Boxes, or . . . was there another word for boxes? Jars. Tins. Okay, six jars in a row. It still made no sense. The word next to the tins—God? What did that mean? She had never heard it before. And why were O and D in G? Idly, she wrote down what she was thinking—'O D in G'. The answer leapt out at her.

'O'ding!' she yelled, then hushed herself quickly. 'Six tins in a row o'ding—six tins o'ding? Six-*teen* o'ding! Got it! But sixteen o'ding *when?*'

She frowned at the picture puzzle below the line. A sock, a dash, and an SK—hmmm. Or was that not a dash at all, but a minus sign? Yes, that worked—so she had OC. Plus T. OCT. Plus an eye. OCTEYE? She shrugged and went on. Plus T. OCTEYET. Octite! Next—33 + 1. Easy—34. Octite 34? Counting up from when? Since the kidnapping of the Tarasuns? Couldn't be—it was now over 60 octites since the Octoversary. She frowned at the numbers again, trying to look at them differently.

What if it wasn't thirty-three, but three three? Or double three? Or two three? Or . . . two times three? She felt a shiver of excitement. Two times three plus one. Seven! Octite 7 of the octoll since they'd arrived in Glo—that was today! She glanced at her dingdial. Ten o'ding! If they didn't 'unstick' the lock of the dungeon in the next six dings, the Marani—and the Rubies—would never be free! That was *so* not fair—by the rules of Taratrap 8.0, they had until tomorrow, the last octite of the octoll, but when had Shaap Azur *ever* played fair?

She had to start heading towards the cell–now!–but *where* was she to go? Where *was* the third riddle? It *must* be somewhere on the cliff path. Maybe the others had already found it. If they hadn't, she would have to tell them to begin looking. She began to race back towards the path.

'Tufan! Get over here—quick!' Zvala sounded frantic. 'The eggs—they are beginning to hatch!'

Tufan sat up groggily. He had tended to the injured Bay Runda through the nite, until his eyes had begun to close against his will. He had fallen into an exhausted sleep by the massive nest, after making the rope fast around it. Now he pushed himself quickly towards Zvala.

Cracks had appeared on the speckled shiny surface of two of the three crimson eggs. An impatient tap-tapping from pairs of tiny beaks sounded from the inside as baby Bays jostled to get out of their spherical prisons. At Zvala and Tufan watched, fascinated, little heads began to poke out, their eyes firmly shut, already screeching for food.

'Awwwww!' whispered Zvala, her arms still around the eggs. 'Say hi to your sort-of mommy, babies!'

'Don't confuse the poor things,' Tufan said sternly. 'Or they'll actually believe you and turn into, like, *totally* loony pink-crested warblers to please you, and then . . . Ow!' Zvala had socked him neatly around the head.

CRACK! With a loud report, the third egg split neatly in half, startling Tufan and sending Zvala leaping out of the nest. Out tumbled a rolled-up palmyra scroll.

Tufan and Zvala goggled. What was this now?

SCREEEECH!

The mother Bay Runda, her wings almost healed, had hoisted herself onto the path and was coming towards them with short, jerky, flying hops, shrieking protectively. Zvala picked up the scroll and hurriedly got out of the way. The Bay Runda perched on the nest, cooing to her babies.

'They'll be okay now,' smiled Tufan. 'Time to get going.'

'Hey! You guys!' Zarpa was waving desperately at them from the edge of the meadow, trying to get their attention. 'Look for another riddle before you get over here—it must be there around you somewhere!'

'Found it!' Zvala waved the scroll. 'You'll never believe where it was!'

❖

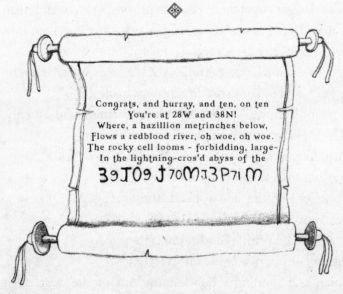

Congrats, and hurray, and ten, on ten
You're at 28W and 38N!
Where, a hazillion metrinches below,
Flows a redblood river, oh woe, oh woe.
The rocky cell looms - forbidding, large-
In the lightning-cros'd abyss of the
ƎϿꞀOϿ Ꞁ70ꟽꓕƷPꓕ ꟽ

Zarpa gulped. 'A river of blood? Whose . . . blood?'

'Glo's, silly! Look around you—the soil is a deep, deep red. So a river flowing through here would look red too, right?' Zarpa looked sheepish. 'What *I'm* more worried about is the "lightning-cros'd abyss"—?'

'It should be way below us—we could figure out exactly where if only we could make sense of this number and letter pattern,' frowned Zvala.

'There's also a strange symbol in the middle,' Zarpa pored over the scroll with Zvala. 'We have to get this quickly,' she glanced anxiously at her dingdial. 'Only five dings to go before the Marani gets locked in forever!'

'Chillax, Captain!' Tufan noisily slurped up the last of the magginoo and spritzed himself liberally with Max deo. Fragrant and sated, he strode towards the girls. 'Make way, make way, for the Mastastic Mind-Unboggler, the Celebrated Cipher-Cracker, the . . .'

' . . . Malodorous Maxphyxiator!' completed Zvala, holding her nose and handing over the scroll. Zarpa giggled—Zvala had turned it upside down to confuse Tufan. 'So, your Stinkiness, what does the pattern mean?'

Tufan picked up the scroll. 'Simple,' he said superiorly. 'As it says here quite clearly, we need to get to Wilderwolf Gorge.' His lips curled in mock-disdain. 'You mean you didn't see it? What's wrong with your oculi, people?'

Zvala's mouth fell open. She grabbed the scroll back and turned it upside down. There it was, clear as anything—Wilderwolf Gorge! High-fiving Tufan, Zarpa clicked on the latlongmeter to locate it.

'The Mastastic Mind-Unboggler,' Tufan bowed elaborately to a steadily-reddening Zvala, 'at your service.'

Fourteen

Beep! 1 New Msg—Taranauts.

Dana handed over her summoner to Dada, completely absorbed in watching Glolite TV's footage of the octite when the Taranauts had first come to Glo. They would only be allowed to starcast the program after she had approved it. There she was, sashaying down the ramp towards them . . . 'No, no, you have to cut this bit out,' she was saying to the Glolite crew. 'I look fat in this, don't I, Dead-Eye?'

Dada shrugged, walked over to Lt Muntri, and clicked the summoner on.

Hedng 4 Wilderwolf Gorge. 5 dngs 2 go bt dedlne. Fngrs xd!

Lt Muntri jumped up from his chair and gestured to his personal bodyguard. 'Have the Chief of Glosafety report to the Marani's office—on the double!' Closely followed by Dada, he strode away in the same direction.

Precisely two dinglings later, with the Chief beside him, Lt Muntri unlocked the door of the Marani's office. Three dinglings later, he unlocked the safe and took out the secure summoner and clicked it on.

No New Msgs.

Lt Muntri clicked on the inbox and opened the last received message. His face went pale.

Hedng 4 Wilderwolf Gorge. 5 dngs 2 go b4 dedlne. Fngrs xd!

'How in Kay Laas . . .? There is *no* way anyone could have got to this summoner and opened the message. And this one has been forwarded too . . .'

The Chief of Glosecurity cleared his throat. 'The Glo Biggabheja Society had a theory, Sir,' he said. 'Remote access. Someone is accessing the secure summoner— *from the outside.*'

'Impossible!' sputtered Lt Muntri. 'This summoner is secure—and password-protected! No one but the Marani and I know the password!'

'Yes, but even the most secure summoner is no match for an ingenious hacker,' explained the Chief. 'And passwords . . .' he hesitated. 'Pardon me for speaking my mind, Sir, but not everyone is very careful about passwords. They may write it down somewhere so they will not forget, or visualize it in their minds, making it easy for anyone good at Stellipathy to intercept it . . .'

Lt Muntri turned red. 'Thank you, Chief,' he snapped. 'Maybe those all-knowing Biggabhejas of yours can make themselves useful by finding out *where* the summoner is being accessed from, and . . .'

The Chief Biggabheja burst through the door. 'We've isolated the remote access signal!' he announced. 'The latlong coordinates are 38N, 28W—somewhere in the region of the Wilderwolf Gorge!'

The three mithyakas in the room looked at each other, thunderstruck. Whoever was accessing the secure summoner was somewhere near the Wilderwolf Gorge, where the Taranauts were headed!

'He-ya,' Dana sashayed into the room, looking worried. 'Dead-Eye, there is a bit of Glolite SV's footage I want your opinion on.'

'Not now, Dana,' Dada said tersely. 'There are more important things to think about right now than how you look on SV.'

'It's not what you are thinking,' said Dana quietly. Her voice had lost its singsong silliness. 'There's something very strange going on, and I want you to see it.'

Dada looked at Dana warily. She looked dead serious, a different girl from the self-obsessed popstar. 'Let's go, then,' he said, following her out of the room.

Beep! 1 New Msg—Undisclosed Sender

Ograzur Dusht ground his teeth. 'Curse the brats— they found all four riddles! But no matter—even if they make it unharmed through the Gorge, which I seriously doubt they will, there is a nice reception waiting for them at the 'rocky cell'. Super work, Dro Hie!'

'Harharazur!' cheered the other Ograzurs at the table. In less than six dings, Mithya could be theirs!

'This looks like a good spot to rapseil down into the canyon from,' said Tufan. 'Wilderwolf Gorge is a little ahead, but the canyon narrows dangerously there. Ready?'

The girls nodded. Helmets, elbow pads and knee pads to protect them if they banged into the canyon walls on the way down—check. Gloves to minimize rope-burn—check. Safety harness—check. 'What setting for the Nanos, Tufan?' called Zarpa. 'Barefoot,' replied Tufan. 'It's the coolest.' When they touched the Barefoot icon, the shoes turned into 'feet', gripping each toe separately—the best grip ever for rock-climbing.

Throwing the ends of their retractable ropes around boulders at the top of the canyon and clipping the rope cases to their waists, the Taranauts took a deep breath and walked carefully backwards off the cliff and into the canyon.

A whole ding later, battered, bruised and scraped, they high-fived each other on the bank of the 'redblood river'. Shucking off their gear, they left it by the hanging ropes—ready for the journey back. Zarpa clicked on her latlongmeter. 'Wilderwolf Gorge begins just around that bend in the river. Hurry, it's 12 o'ding already!'

The Taranauts moved as swiftly as they could over the

rough, rocky terrain, munching bits of their Born-Again Bars. Half past 12 and the bend had not yet been gained! They quickened their pace, conscious that they also had to conserve their energy for whatever awaited them in the 'lightning-cros'd abyss'.

'Almost there!' called Zarpa, racing for the bend, as she stole a quick look at her dingdial. 13 o'ding!

Turning the corner, she stood still, taking stock. Ahead of her, the canyon narrowed, its steep, high walls closing in around the river from both sides.

OOOOAAUUUU! With a caterwaul that made her hair stand on end, a bolt of lightning zigzagged across the gorge, its brilliant white light bouncing off the canyon walls, throwing the silver tantrite rocks that lined them into sharp relief. Zarpa screamed.

The next dingling, Zvala and Tufan were by her side. 'What is it?' Zvala's voice was shaky. 'What was that sound?' Zarpa pointed a trembling finger upwards. 'I can't see anyth . . .' began Tufan, struggling to see in the dim Taralite. Lightning streaked across the canyon again from another direction, its high-pitched wail cutting him off. In the sudden brightness, Zvala and Tufan saw what Zarpa had just seen, and froze. Near the top of the canyon, their silver fur bristling as they prepared to leap down the canyon walls towards the Taranauts, were a dozen snarling wilderwolves!

Dada, Lt Muntri and the Chief of Glosafety stared intently at the starvision screen as the Glolite crew ran their last few minutes of footage. In the distance, through a haze of red dust, they could see Bulletbikes flying into the air as Tufan got to work, and hear the swish-swish-SMACK of the Silambalati sticks of the Marani's guards as they made contact with the bikers. A burst of fire on the far right of the screen pinpointed Zvala's location. A little red whirlwind tore towards the motionframe—Zarpa.

'Now!' Dana got to her feet. 'Slow it down, please. Dead-Eye, Lt Muntri, look closely at the Bulletbikes on the right side of the screen.'

Three Bulletbikes appeared on the screen, heading away from the chaos of the battlefield. On the flanking bikes were two mithyakas in black, their faces obscured by their mirrored helmets. Riding between the two, her pant suit a crimson gash against the black-and-silver Bulletbike, her signature mehenna-streaked hair billowing out behind her in a scarlet cloud, was the smiling Marani of Glo!

'The Marani, *my* Marani—she was not kidnapped after all,' whispered Lt Muntri. He clutched the arms of his chair for support, utterly broken. The Chief of Glosafety sat down suddenly, looking equally stunned.

'The dirty traitor!' Dada was shaking with rage. '*She* has been the one accessing the secure summoner from her 'cell'—and keeping her Downsider friends up to date! Send the Taranauts a message now, Dana—tell them to stay away from Wilderwolf Gorge!'

Dana's fingers flew over her summoner keypad. A dingling later, the message was returned. *Recipient unreachable.*

Dada stood up, his face a mask of worry. 'The Taranauts need us, but we're never going to get to Pur Butte in time. Never!' His voice rose in panic.

'Never say never,' said a cheery voice from the door. 'I happen to know a little trick to get you anywhere you need to at the speed of thought. Care to try it?'

Dada whirled. 'The aquauto driver! Zub, right?'

'That's what they call me,' Zub bowed.

'My little brother adores you,' said Dada, shaking Zub's hand warmly. 'And any friend of Tufan's is a friend of mine. Lead the way!'

'Count me in!' squealed Dana. 'What's the little trick?'

'It's called Stelliportation,' winked Zub. '"The transfer of matter from one point to another, without the matter traversing the intervening space in material form", if you want the lexpad definition.'

'Like, what-*ever*,' Dana rolled her eyes. 'Will it hurt?'

'It *is* a little disorienting at first,' admitted Zub. 'But there's a whole bunch of us going, so it won't be so bad. They're all waiting outside. We have the Glo-Getters, of course,' Dada pumped his fists in the air with delight, 'there's a dozen minimits from Lustr, and a certain champion Lunascoot Latangler from Sparkl . . .'

Outside, everyone piled into Zub's blue-and-silver aquauto, which seemed suddenly able to accommodate them all. 'Hold hands, everyone,' yelled Zub. 'Close your eyes. Focus on the words "Pur Butte", "see" the mountains in your head! Channel your energies, and wish harder than you've ever wished in your life that you were there now. Harder, *harder* . . .' The aquauto juddered.

'Hey! Hey you! What do you think you are doing?' The Chief of Glosafety, realizing he had lost control of the situation, came running towards the aquauto.

'Let's do it for the Taranauts!' roared Zub urgently. 'For the Rubies, for Glo, for Mithya!' The aquauto began to hum. The street outside, and the Chief himself, began to blur and dissolve. 'And aw-a-y-y-y-y we go!

Fifteen

The Taranauts huddled together in terror, ears straining for the skittering of claws on rock, noses primed for the stench of moldy wilderwolf breath. Nothing. *OOOAAAAUUUU!* Zvala jumped. Lightning lit up the gorge again, the bolt striking the ground almost at their feet. The Taranauts looked up fearfully. The wilderwolves were still there, still frozen in mid-lunge. 'It's okay, guys,' Zarpa laughed shakily. 'They aren't real.'

'But they are just as dangerous as real ones,' warned Tufan. 'Looks like these guys have whopper lightning hurlers fitted into their mouths, and I'm betting those are motion-sensitive—watch this!' He chucked what was left of his Born-Again Bar into the air. SIZZZLE! A white-hot blast fried the bar to a sooty crisp even before it had hit the ground!

'Oh-*kay*,' Zvala mouthed, not daring to move a muscle. 'Now what?'

'Sit down and think!' mouthed Tufan.

'There's no way we can get across the gorge,' sighed Zarpa a whole ding later, after a series of unsuccessful experiments. 'Face it—we have failed.'

Zvala looked up at the wilderwolves. 'See, the wilderwolves' heads are all angled downwards,' she said. 'If only we could go *over* them somehow . . . .'

'Blah-de-blah-de-blah,' Tufan trawled through his pockets, looking for a brainchow bar. 'You've said that only a mazillion times before, sillyk . . . .' He stopped, frowning, as his fingers closed around something unfamiliar. He drew it out. 'My crittercaller!' he cried, slapping his forehead. 'Maybe we *can* go over the wilderwolves!' Quickly, he scrolled down the menu, until he came to Hakibyrd, Endangered. The Bay Runda was first on the list. Tufan clicked on it, raised the crittercaller to his lips and blew. SCREEEEECH!

Five dinglings passed, then ten. 'Maybe she's too far away,' said Zvala. 'Maybe she's too busy with the babies,' sighed Zarpa, crestfallen. Ignoring them, Tufan blew the caller one more time. SCREEEECH!

SCREEEEEECH! A giant winged shape glided over the edge of the precipice, blotting out the Taralite and casting the canyon into deep shadow. It hovered there uncertainly, its two heads peering into the gorge.

'Wooohooo!' yelled Tufan, jumping and waving furiously. Hazillion-watvolt heat beams scorched the ground at their feet as the lightning hurlers came alive. Tufan stopped jumping. 'Here, girl, we're down here! Zvala, get some light going so she can see us!'

Flapping its great wings, the Bay Runda dived, swooping unerringly towards the light. The Taranauts plastered themselves to the canyon walls, shading their eyes against the red dust storm, flinching as the gale tore at their hair and clothes. The next dingling, the hakibyrd had coasted to a smooth landing in front of them. She made a grand sight as she stood there, legs stradding the redblood river, fuschia-blue plumage glimmering in the faraway light, cooing at her mithyakin babies.

Tufan clambered up her back first, speaking to her gently and pointing to their destination—the other side of the gorge. Zvala and Zarpa scrambled up behind him, sinking at every step into the deep-pile feather carpet. 'Hold tight now!' Tufan called over his shoulder. 'You can clutch and pull at her feathers all you want—she won't even feel it. And stay low—we *will* be blitzed for the first couple of dinglings, until we rise out of range!'

With another ear-splitting screech, the Bay Runda rose into the air. The Taranauts ducked, terrified, as the hurlers, with a cacophony of yowling, unleashed a barrage of lightning bolts at the hakibyrd. Amazingly, the lightning did very little damage, ricocheting harmlessly off the Bay Runda's feathers with sharp metallic pings.

'Three . . . two . . . one . . . *and we're out of range!*
Yayyyyyyy! The Taranauts are back in business!' Tufan
punched the air with his fists and nearly fell off. Hurriedly,
he grabbed the Bay Runda's neck again, pretending not
to notice the girls giggling behind him.

The hakibyrd began to soar out of the gorge. 'Hey,
not so high, girl! We need to find the Marani—just skim
the top of the gorge. Zarpa, the durdekscope!'

Zarpa raised her durdekscope to her eyes and
scanned the gorge in sweeping arcs. On her fifth pass,

she found it. 'There! I see her! There's this deep, deep hollow in the rock, and it's all barred on the top—she's in it! We only have a few dinglings left—go, girl!'

'She's going to dive!' yelled Tufan. 'Get set for the wildest hovercarpet ride of your life!'

The Bay Runda folded its wings and plunged into a vertical dive, dropping like a stone. The wind whipped past the Taranauts' ears. Shrieking with excitement, they held on for dear life.

Suddenly, another Bay Runda appeared from below, screeching for all it was worth, heading straight for them! It was even bigger than the one they were riding, its plumage a riotous indigo and gold—a male!

The female Bay Runda swerved to avoid a collision, so sharply that the Taranauts almost slid off her back. Then it began to fly wingtip to wingtip with the male, obediently following where it led. Two dinglings later, both hakibyrds came to rest on a grassy plateau above the Marani's cell.

'What was all *that* about?' Tufan sounded annoyed. 'We were almost there and then . . .'

'He-*ya*, Taranauts!' The Taranauts stared. A tall, twig-thin girl was sashaying towards them like a model down a runway, her knee-length pink-purple hair in two high panditails on either side of her head.

Zvala shook her head to clear it. That wasn't . . . it couldn't be . . . Dana? But it was! A whole bunch of their friends had appeared at the other end of the plateau. They greeted the Taranauts with a glad cry, and raced towards them—Dada, a dozen other Glokos holding Bel Nolo sticks like they were Silambalatis, the minimits, and was that . . . Mog Ambow? They all looked a little bruised, a little bloody, but otherwise in good spirits.

'Wha . . .?' choked Zarpa. 'How . . . how did you get here? And *why*?'

'Zub brought us,' said Dada, looking around him. 'He was here just a moment ago. As to why, you will find out later. Now,' Dada's face grew solemn, 'listen to me carefully and do *exactly* as I say. The Marani's cell is just below us. Get there and unlock it—the key is hanging right by it. That will release the Rubies. *Then lock the cell again, before the Marani can get out.*'

The Taranauts stared at Dada as if he was nuts. 'Just *do* it—it's very, very important!' Dada looked so severe that Zarpa nodded. 'Yes, sir!' she mumbled. 'Ten dinglings to the deadline—hurry!'

Precisely eight dinglings later, against the background noise of the shrieking curses of a traitorous Marani, the sky over Pur Butte burst into brilliant vermilion light as the Rubies returned to Tara, the supersun of Mithya.

Sixteen

The Taranauts sat at the conference table in what used to be the Marani of Glo's office, stunned. Dada, Dana, Zub, the Chief of Glosafety, the Chief Glo Biggabheja, Mog Ambow, and Lt. Muntri—the newly-appointed Maraza of Glo, had just filled them in on the chain of events that had led to Dada, Dana and the rest of the Glokos landing up at Pur Butte so unexpectedly.

'Wow!' breathed Tufan. 'That was so touch-and-go. If you hadn't got there when you did . . . .'

'We would have gotten there earlier,' muttered Mog Ambow, who had defected to the Emperaza's camp, 'but the place was crawling with the Marani's goons, and they put up a stiff fight.'

'Ah, *that* explains it,' grinned Tufan, thinking of the odd way in which the Glo-Getters were holding their sticks.

'Uffpah, if that Bay Runda hadn't come at us like a rocket, we would have gone straight to the cell. Where *did* he come from, anyway?'

Dada shrugged who knows. 'What if,' said Zvala, 'What if,' said Zvala, 'Dana hadn't been watching Glolite SV's footage that carefully . . .'

'Or if you guys hadn't decided that the Bay Runda and her eggs were important . . .' put in Zub.

'Or if you hadn't gone over to Dada's dorm and brought him here in the first place . . .' said Zarpa. They were all silent for a moment, thinking.

'Um, Lt. Muntri,' said Dana at last, 'can we do, like, a timeout?'

'Of course, Dana,' said the new Maraza. 'I apologize— you must all want to rest.'

'I don't know about everyone else,' said Dana, winking at Zvala. 'But Firegirl and I have plans.'

Zarpa shot Zvala a hurt look—was Zvala going to abandon her all over again?

Zvala grinned at Dana, her eyes twinkling. 'You bet!'

Before anyone knew what was happening, they had pounced—Zvala on Zarpa, and Dana on a very surprised Tufan. 'Dana's got it all set up,' chortled Zvala, pinning Zarpa down. 'Makeover time, you two!'

'Noooooooo!' yelled Zarpa and Tufan as Zvala and Dana dragged them from the room, kicking and screaming.

Shuk Tee closed the detailed report on the rescue of the Rubies that she had received that morning from Lt. Muntri. Her face was grim.

The battle was getting fiercer, coming closer home. This time, it had been the Marani of Glo who had switched loyalties, next time, it could be *anyone*. The battle was also getting *smarter*—the enemy was getting better at the planning, more organized, more ingenious.

The Marani's scheme to send an SV crew out with the Taranauts, to keep them under constant supervision, for instance. Or the plan to rope in Dana Suntana, idolized by at least one of the Taranauts. The giz wizardry—which, of course, had always been Shaap Azur's forte—involved in hacking secure summoners to allow remote access.

Luckily, the Marani's first plan had failed, when the Taranauts had rejected the reality show idea. But the very next morning, three other summoners, also programmed like Dana's, had magically appeared!

She frowned, and picked up the report again, flipping through it until she had found the page she wanted. She re-read it slowly. The summoners, Lt. Muntri wrote, had been sent from Kay Laas.

A chill ran down Shuk Tee's spine. She herself hadn't signed off on any such package, and she was almost certain the Emperaza hadn't either. Who, then, had sent the summoners from Kay Laas?